DRAGON BALL

Is This the End?

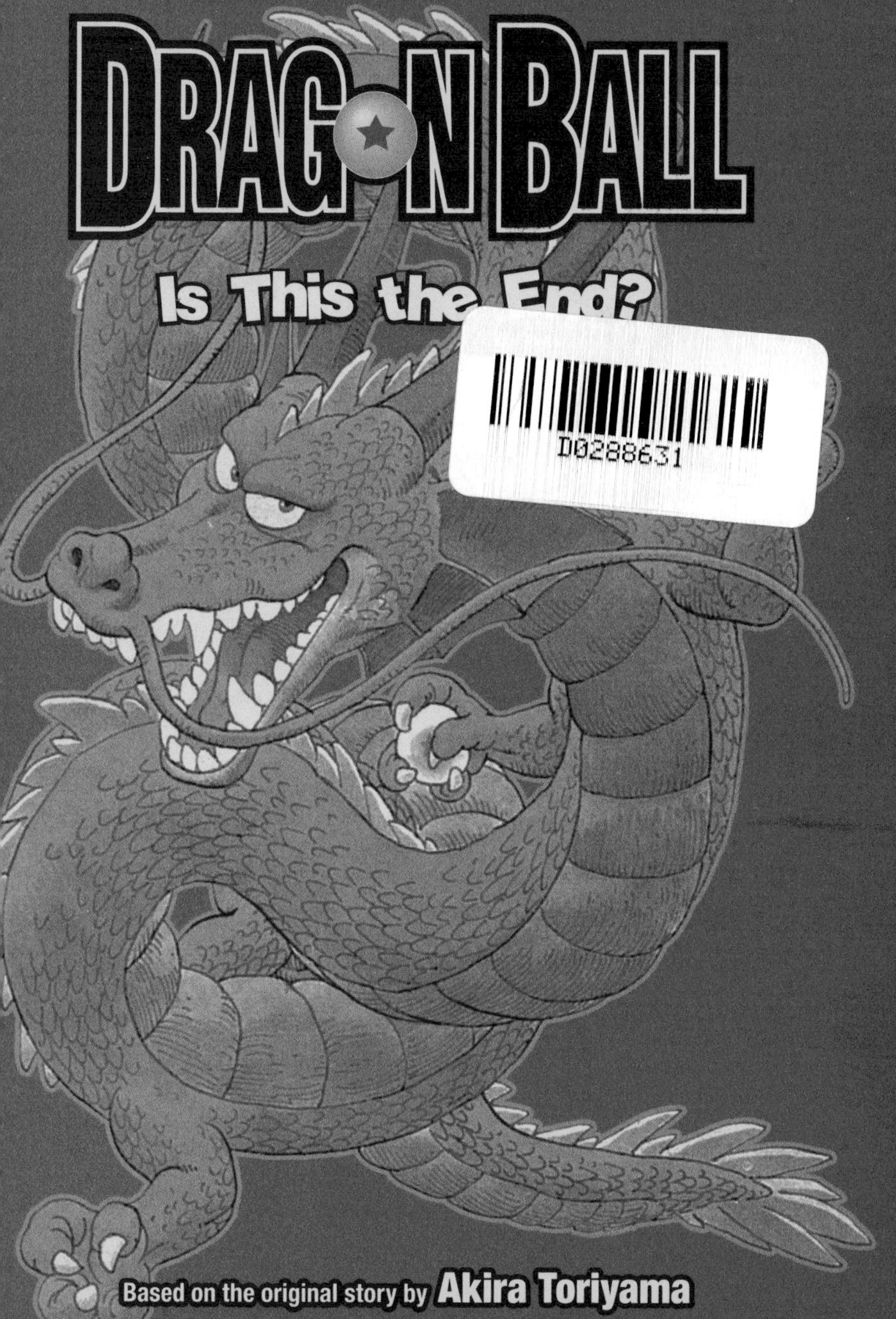

Based on the original story by **Akira Toriyama**

Adapted by Gerard Jones

DRAGON BALL IS THIS THE END?
CHAPTER BOOK 9

Illustrations: Akira Toriyama
Design: Frances O. Liddell
Coloring: ASTROIMPACT, Inc.
Touch-Up: Frances O. Liddell & Walden Wong
Original Story: Akira Toriyama
Adaptation: Gerard Jones

Sources for page 78, "A Note About Namu":

Shukavak N. Dasa. "Religious Marks: Tilaka/Tika" in *A Hindu Primer*.
http://www.sanskrit.org/www/Hindu%20Primer/religiousmarks.html (Accessed March 2, 2010)

Subhaniy Das. "Hinduism for Beginners." *About.com: Hinduism*.
http://hinduism.about.com/od/basics/p/hinduismbasics.htm (Accessed March 2, 2010)

Subhaniy Das. "An Illustrated Primer of Hinduism for Children." *About.com: Hinduism*.
http://hinduism.about.com/od/hinduismforkids/ig/Hinduism-A-to-Z-for-Children/T-for-Tilaka.htm (Accessed March 2, 2010)

Wikimedia Foundation contributors, "Hinduism," Wikimedia Foundation,
http://en.wikipedia.org/wiki/Hinduism#Concept_of_God (Accessed March 2, 2010)

Wikimedia Foundation contributors, "Tilaka," Wikimedia Foundation,
http://en.wikipedia.org/wiki/Tilaka (accessed March 2, 2010).

Printed in the U.S.A.

Published by
VIZ Media, LLC
P.O. Box 77010
San Francisco, CA 94107

10 9 8 7 6 5 4 3 2 1
First printing, July 2010

www.vizkids.com   www.viz.com

Contents

Who's Who

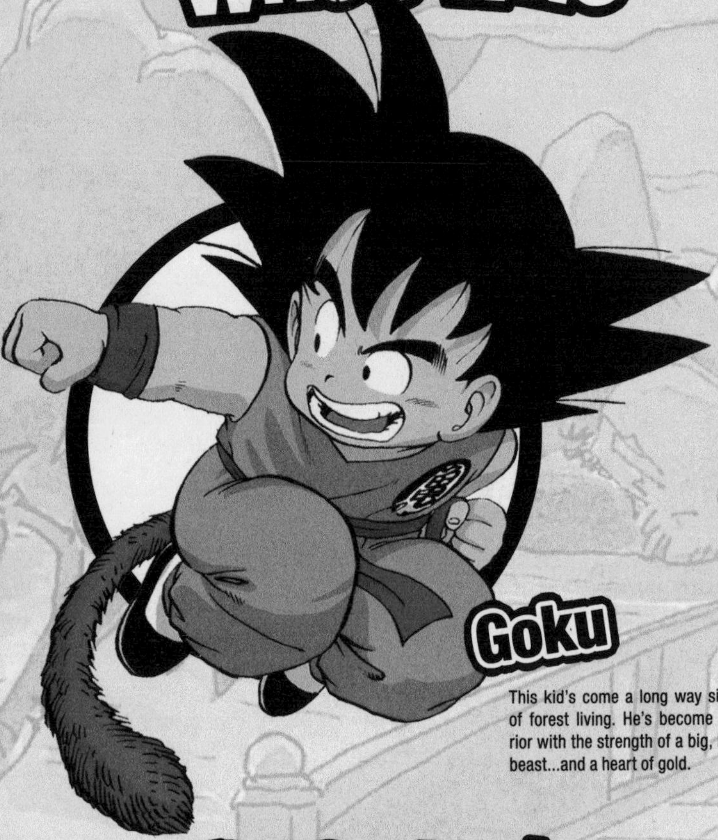

Goku

This kid's come a long way since his days of forest living. He's become quite a warrior with the strength of a big, hairy, apelike beast...and a heart of gold.

The Contenders

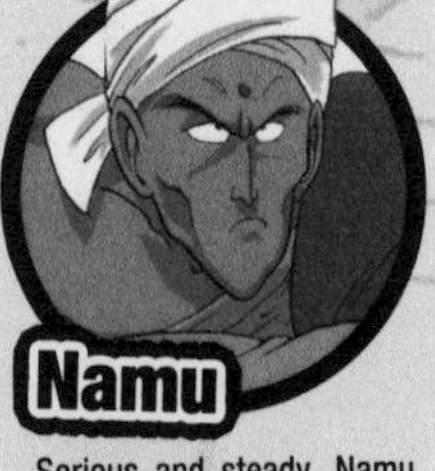

Namu

Serious and steady, Namu has more on his mind than just being named Strongest Under the Heavens.

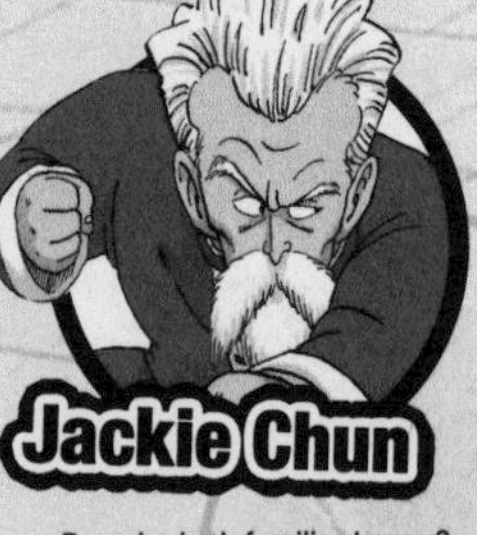

Jackie Chun

Does he look familiar to you?

Bulma, Oolong, Pu'ar

It's Goku's old friends from the days of the Dragon Ball quest! Now they're living in the city, and Oolong has finally taken the underpants off his head.

Master Roshi
a.k.a. Turtle Guy

Master Roshi may look like a harmless old man, but behind that mustache he packs a serious Kame-Hame-Ha!

Yamcha

The bad boy of the desert is back! And this time he's looking a little more tame. He may have lost his bark, but does his Fist of the Wolf Fang still have its bite?

Krillin

This little baldie was full of mischief when he first arrived on Master Roshi's island, but now he's a powerful fighter and Goku's best friend.

What's Happenin'

There are only three fighters left: Goku, Namu, and Jackie Chun. Whoever is eliminated in the next fight will battle Jackie Chun for the championship!

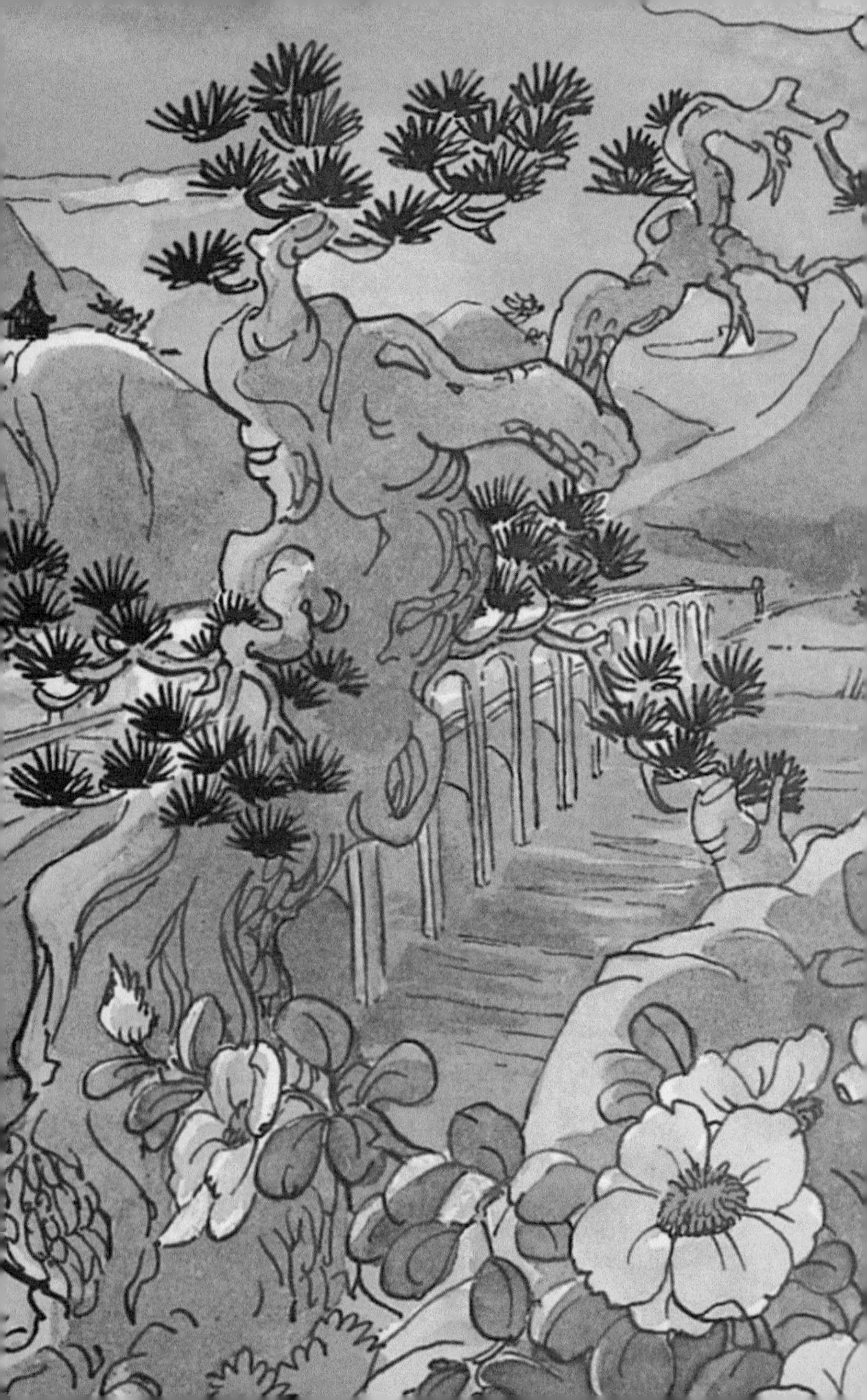

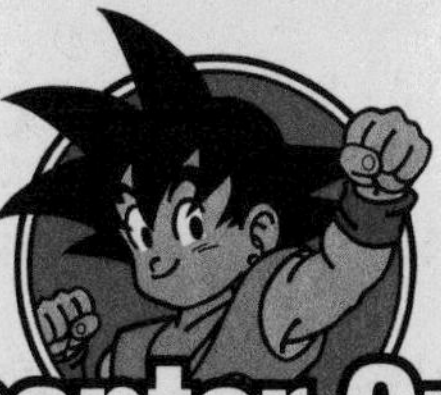

Chapter One

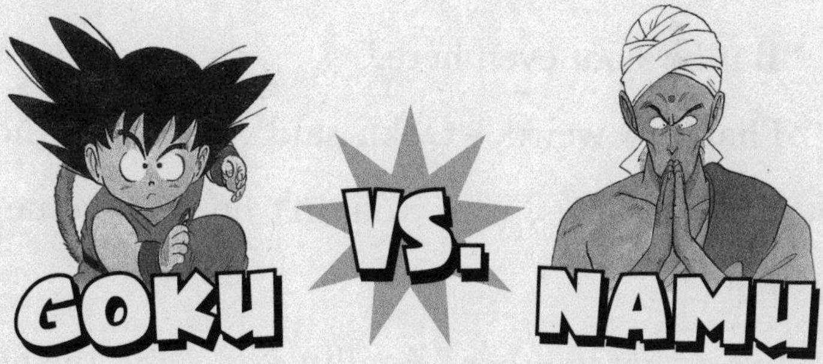
GOKU
VS.
NAMU

The stadium shook with the cheers of thousands of fans. People had come from every land to watch the greatest fighters in the world compete for the title of Strongest Under the Heavens. Now there were only two more matches still to fight!

Krillin and Yamcha made it to the finals, but both had lost their matches. Goku was still in the running. If he could defeat the tall, silent Namu, he would advance to the final match—and face the mysterious Jackie Chun for the championship.

"You've got to take it all, Goku," Krillin said. "Win it for me! Make up for my loss to that Jackie guy! You're the only fighter who's good enough!"

"You think so?" Goku asked.

"Well, except Master Roshi, of course," Krillin said. "But he's not even here."

"That's so weird," Goku said. "After all those months teaching us, why wouldn't he even come to see us fight?"

"I don't get it either," Krillin said. "But the next time I see him, I want to be able to tell him that one of his students is the Strongest Under the Heavens— even if it's not me!"

Just then the announcer's voice filled the air: "Match 6 is about to begin! Contestants Goku and Namu…come to the arena!"

"Welp," Goku said, "guess I'd better go. I hope Namu is fun to fight!"

"Don't have *too* much fun," Krillin said. "Just *beat* him!"

Goku strode onto the stage and warmed up. Namu stared at Goku with cold concentration.

"Hmph," Goku said. "He doesn't *look* like much fun."

Namu wasn't there for fun. All he could think about was the prize money and how the water it would buy would save his village from the terrible drought. No one wanted to win the tournament more desperately than Namu.

The crowd couldn't wait for the fight to begin. Bulma, Oolong, and Pu'ar pushed their way to the front to cheer Goku on.

"You can do it!" Oolong called.

"Dinner's on you if you win!" Bulma yelled.

"You said it!" Goku called back.

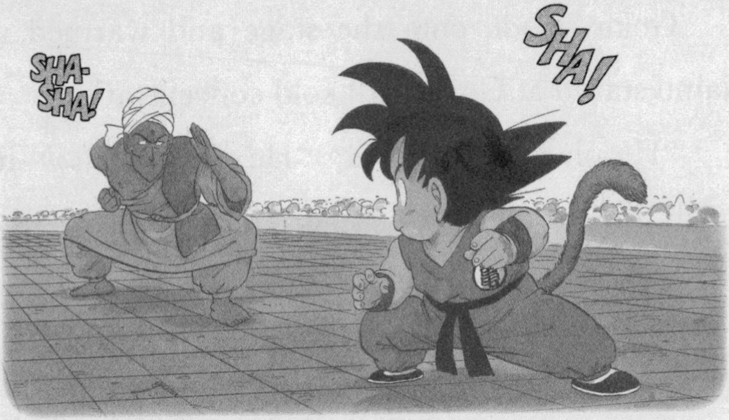
SHA!
SHA-SHA!

At last the announcer made his announcement: "Match 6...BEGIN!!!"

Instantly, Namu assumed a fighting stance and waited for Goku to make the first move.

I think I'll try that move Jackie used to take Krillin down, Goku thought. He grinned at Namu. Then he moved so quickly he became a blur, as if he were both there and not there.

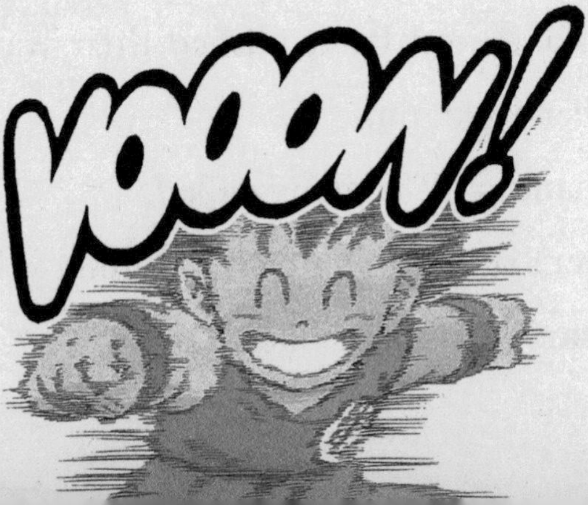
VOOON!

Namu, completely confused, didn't move. He closed his eyes, gritted his teeth, and concentrated. He could feel Goku moving even though he couldn't see him.

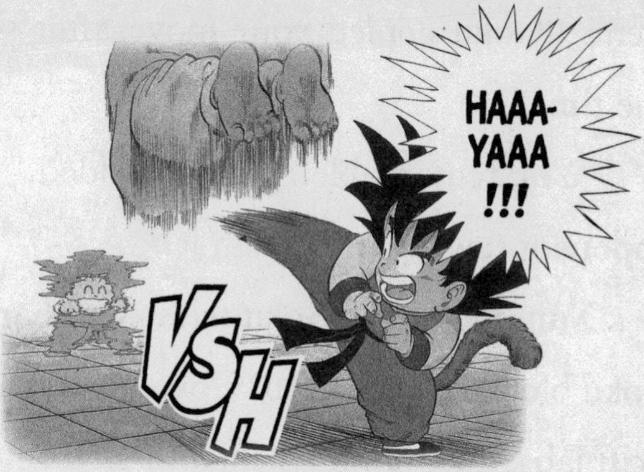
HAAA-
YAAA
!!!
VSH

Suddenly, Goku appeared behind Namu and tried to land a swift kick. But Namu was ready. He leapt out of the way just in time. On the way back down, Namu pushed one foot forward, preparing to slam Goku with a kick of his own. Goku backflipped out of the way.

Shoot! Goku thought. *I thought I did Jackie's move pretty good!*

The two fighters recovered and squared off again.

Yamcha and Jackie Chun watched from the sidelines.

"Did you see that?" Yamcha cried in astonishment. "Goku copied your move after seeing it just one time!"

"Yes, remarkable," Jackie nodded. "Too bad his opponent saw right through it."

Namu came at Goku with two sharp kicks, but Goku blocked them both. Goku answered with three swift jabs, but Namu blocked them all.

"I don't like the looks of this," Krillin said. "They're too evenly matched..."

Namu kicked again and landed a blow to Goku's head. But as Goku went down he swept Namu's feet out from under him with a kick of his own. For an instant Goku had the advantage—he punched Namu and sent him flying toward a far arena wall!

But Namu was too quick. Whipping his body around at the last possible instant, he bounced off the wall and shot straight back at Goku. He slammed

Goku in the back of the neck with a swift chop, and Goku crumpled to the floor. Namu lunged.

"You're going out of bounds *now*!" Namu cried. "This match is *mine*!"

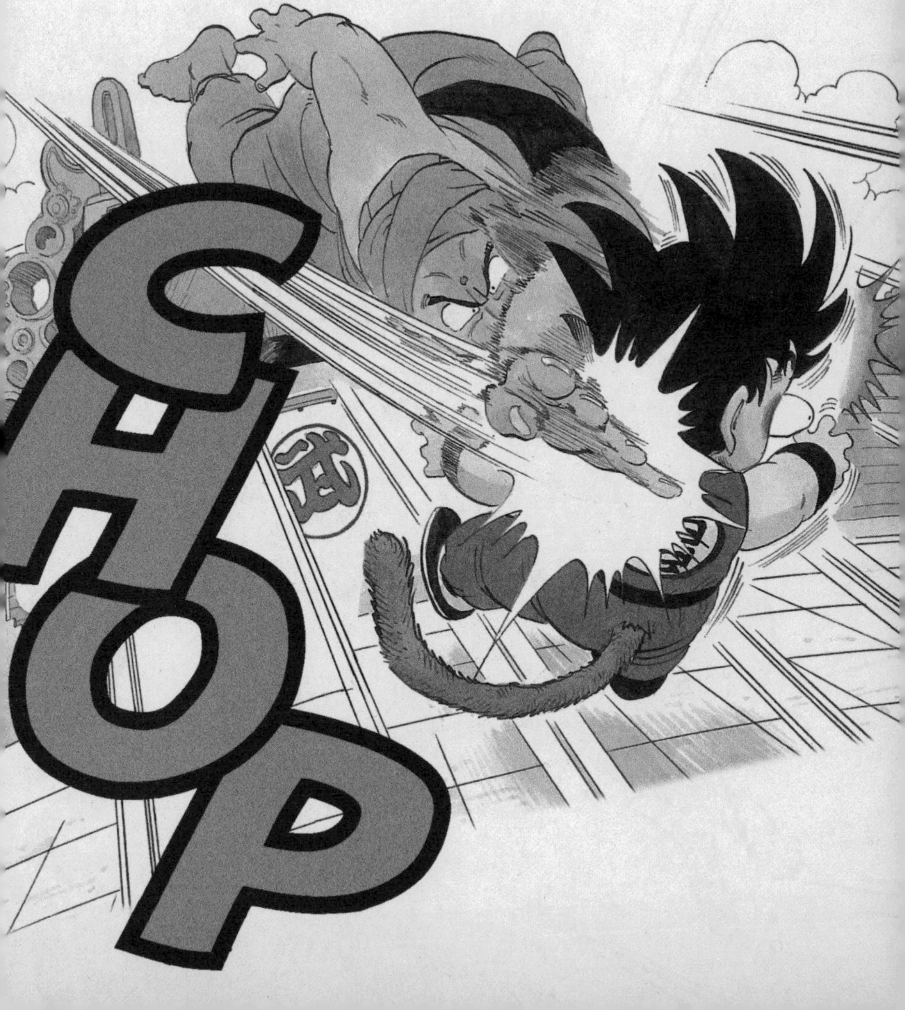
CHOP

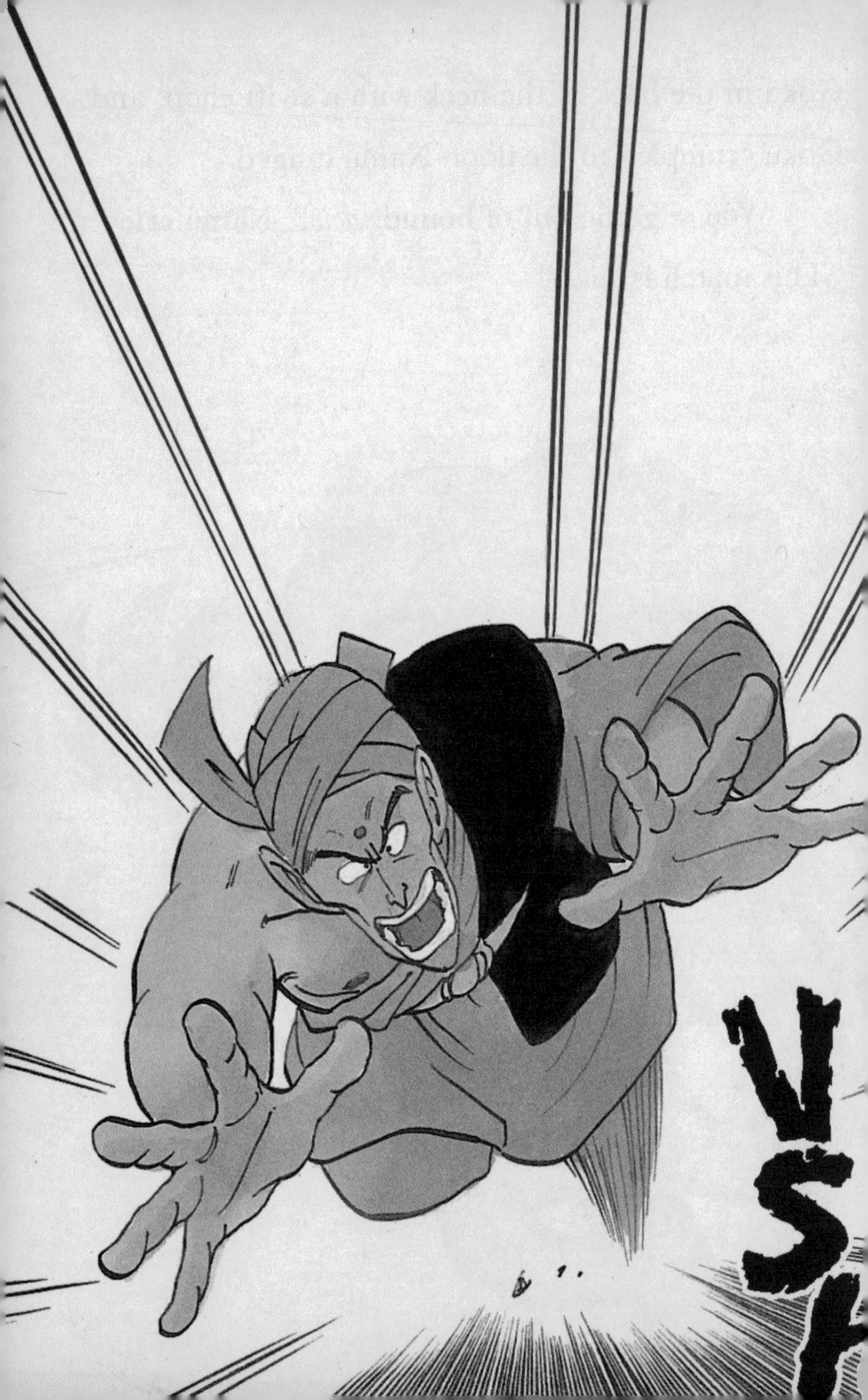
VS

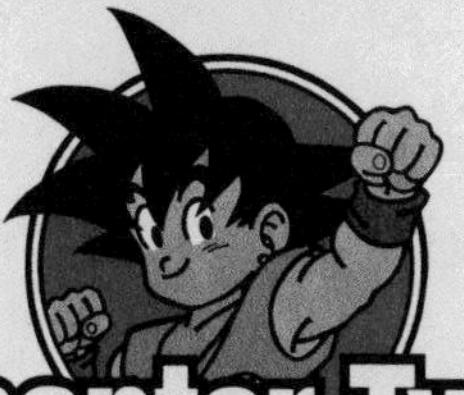

Chapter Two

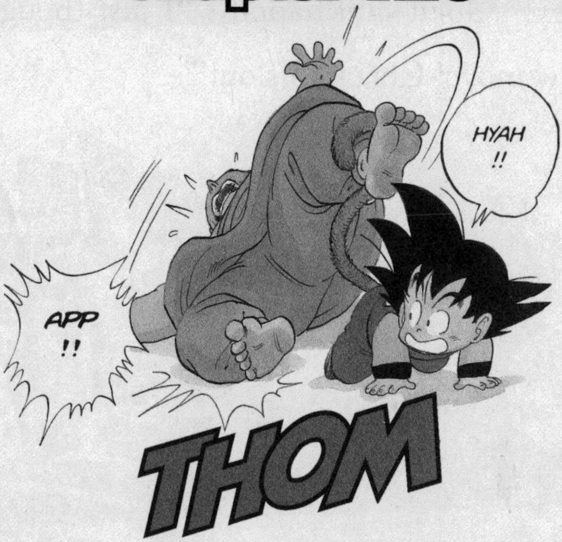
HYAH !!
APP !!
THOM

Goku quickly spun around. With his tail, he reached for Namu's ankle. Namu fell flat on his back.

"You...you have a tail," Namu gasped, "like a monkey!"

"Don'tcha wish you did?" Goku grinned.

"Get him now, Goku!" Krillin yelled. "Get him while he's down!"

But Goku just waited as Namu rose to his feet and took his fighting stance. *What else can I try?* he thought. *Oh!*

"Hey!" Goku said happily. "I just thought of a great new move! Check this out!"

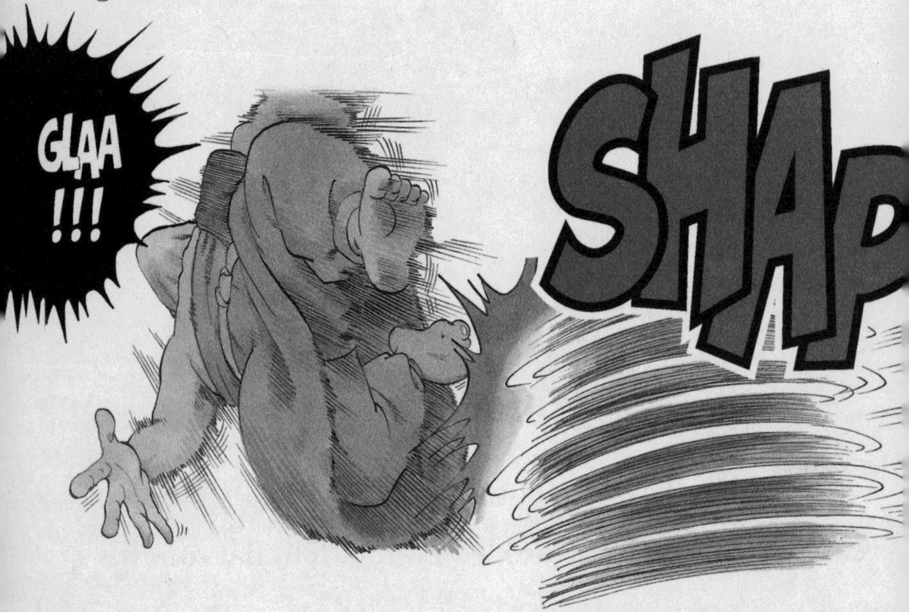
SHAP
GLAA !!!

He started to spin. Around and around, faster and faster, until he looked like a small tornado.

"What? What? *What*?!" Namu cried. As he stood there, the Goku tornado slammed into him, sending Namu flying to the edge of the arena.

It's too powerful, Namu thought, gritting his teeth. *I can't let it touch me again!*

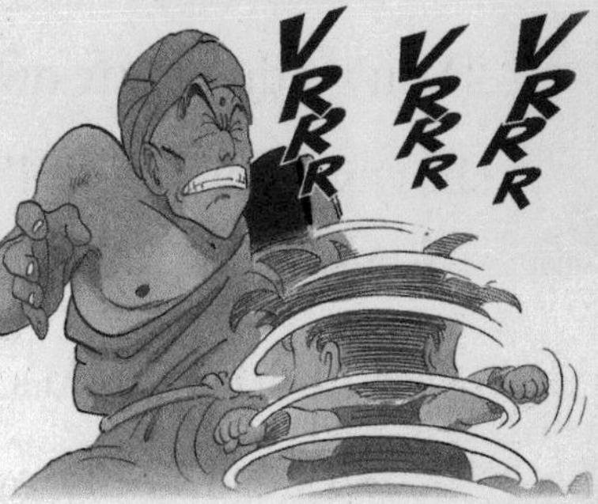
VRRR
VRRR
VRRR

But Goku kept coming. Namu dodged one way, then another. Suddenly he was at the very edge of the arena. One more step and he would be out of bounds.

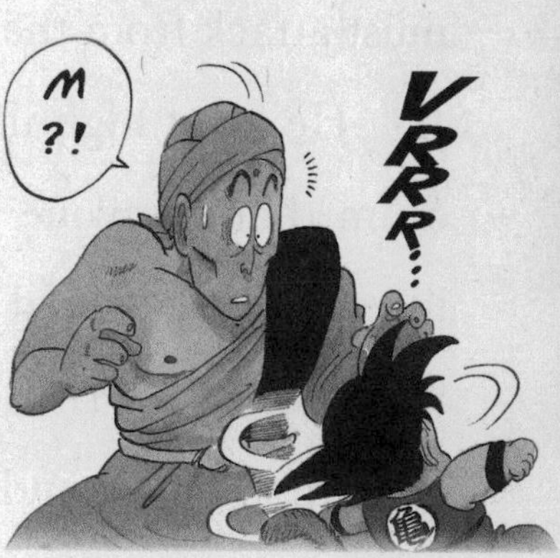
VRRR...
M
?!

"There's nothing I can do!" Namu wailed. "I've lost!" He squeezed his eyes shut and prepared for the final blow.

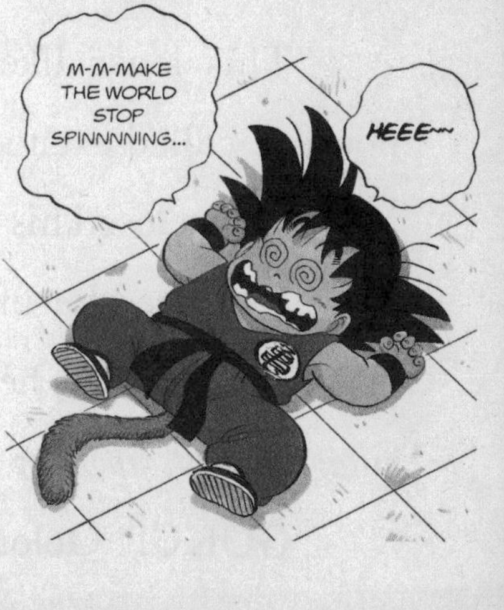
M-M-MAKE THE WORLD STOP SPINNNNING...
HEEE~~

Suddenly, Goku's spinning slowed. He staggered around the stage until he finally fell forward, face first. He looked a little green.

"Ohhhh," he said. "I think I'm gonna throw up."

Namu stood over Goku and clenched his fists. "You've dug your own grave," he said quietly. "I can show you no mercy!"

He prepared to kick Goku out of bounds, but remembered Goku's tail and thought better of it.

"There's only one way to end this," he cried. "I must attack from the sky!"

He leapt high into the air, so far above the stadium that everyone had to crane their necks to see him. Namu hovered in the sky for a moment. Then he crossed his wrists in front of him and plummeted, head first. Faster and faster he fell–aiming straight at Goku.

"This looks like the end for Goku!" the announcer called excitedly.

Namu closed his eyes. He was falling so fast now he was a mere blur in the sky.

Forgive me, lad, he thought, *but I have no choice. My village depends upon my victory!*

"GOKU!" Oolong cried. "GET UP!"

Goku opened his eyes slowly, but it was too late.

Namu was upon him. The full weight of his body slammed into Goku's neck.

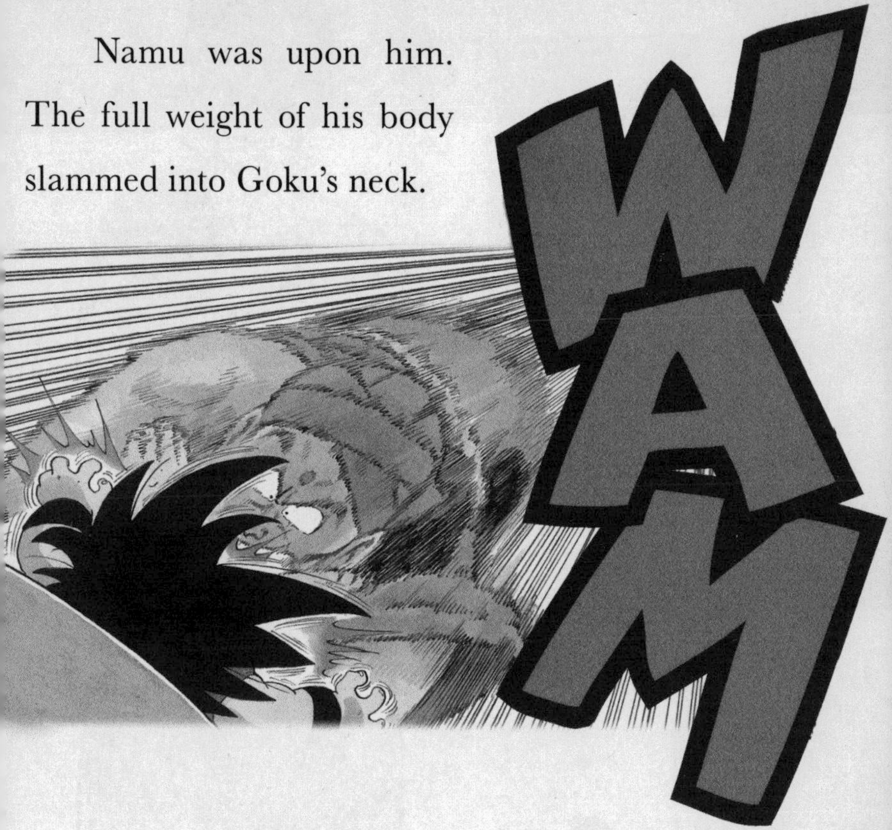
WAM

Goku gasped. And didn't move.

Namu recovered from the fall and stood calmly with his eyes closed. He turned to the announcer and softly said, "You may begin the count."

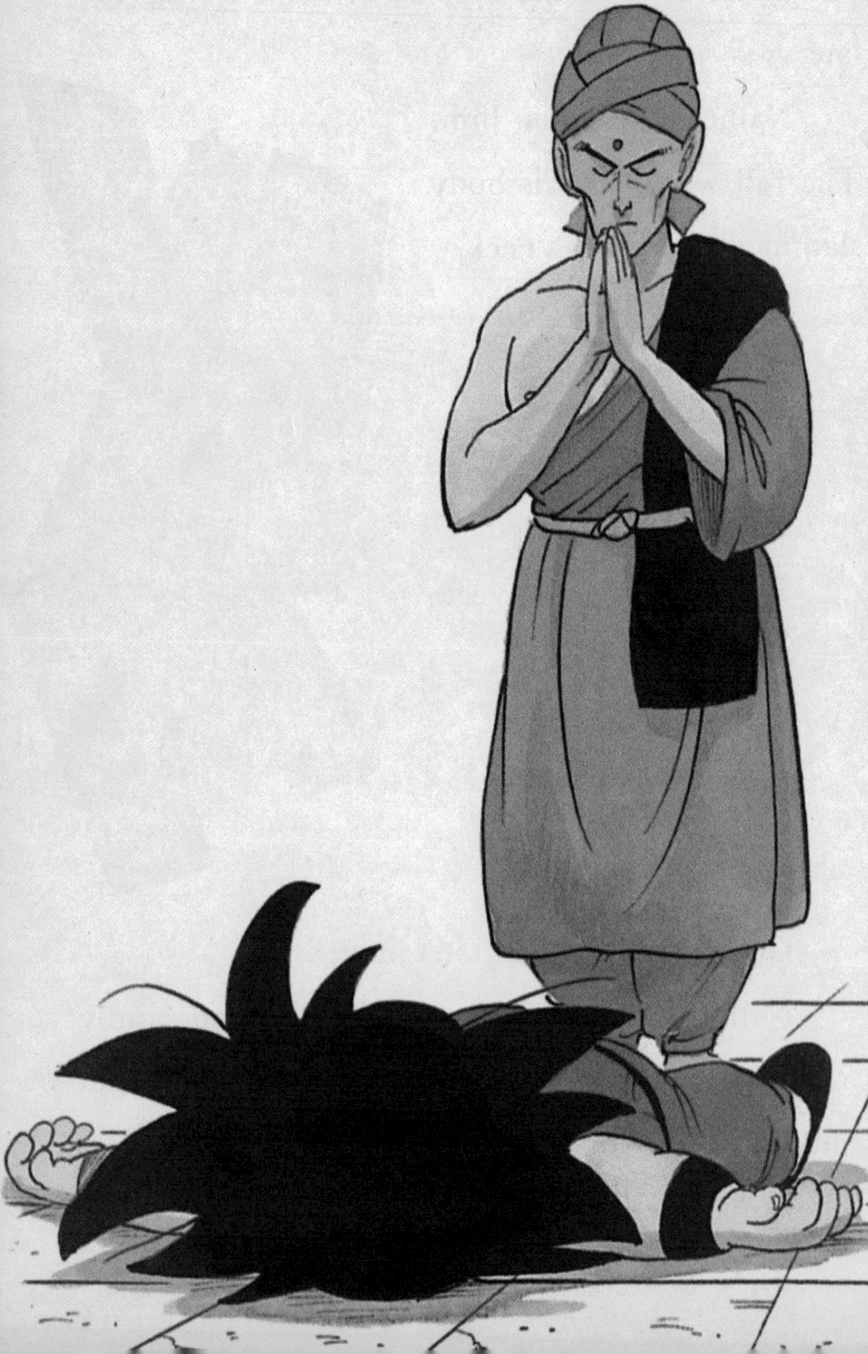

Chapter Three

"H-he took that full force," Yamcha gasped.

"He'll be lucky to live," Jackie agreed.

"I am a peaceful man," Namu replied, over-hearing. "I would not kill. But it will take him at least three days to recover from that blow."

The announcer's count was up to six now, and Goku still hadn't stirred.

"I can't believe he lost," Oolong whispered.

"Seven…eight…nine…"

And then…was that…? *Yes!* The slightest twitch of Goku's finger! And before the announcer could say "ten," Goku was back on his feet.

"What?" Namu cried.

"YES!" Krillin shouted.

Goku brought his hands to his throat and coughed. "That really coulda *hurt*!" he said hoarsely.

The announcer gasped. The crowd cheered. Namu shrieked.

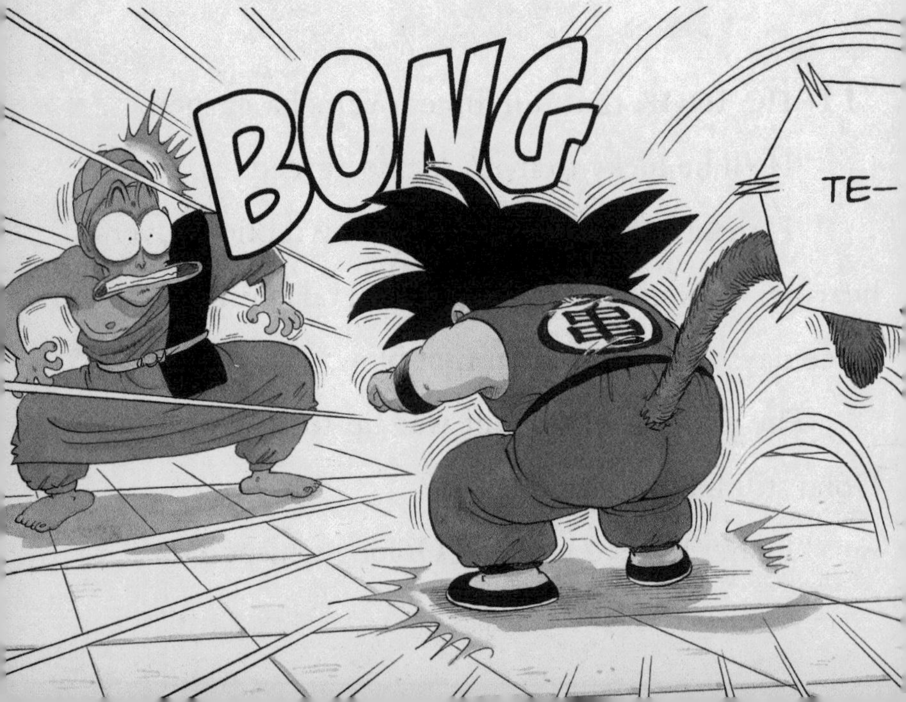
TE–
BONG

"It-it can't *be*!" he screamed. "No mortal being would still be on his feet after a blow like that! Unless..."

Goku cracked his neck a couple of times and shook his shoulders.

"Perhaps I missed the pressure points," Namu said, watching. "I won't make that mistake twice. It's time to end this match!"

With that he rocketed into the sky once more.

"Hey!" Goku cried, watching Namu soar higher and higher until he was just a tiny point. "Cool trick! My turn!"

Goku crouched low and pushed himself into the air.

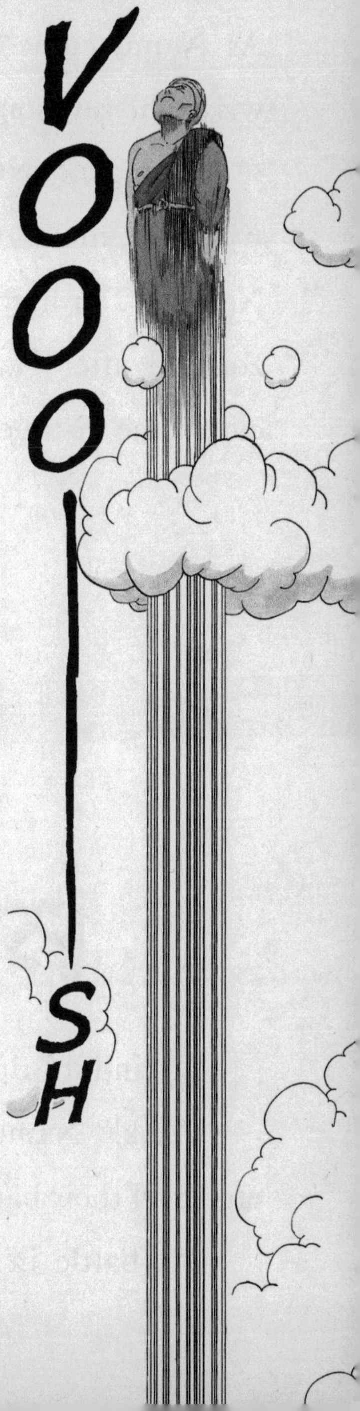
VOOOSH

As Namu came shooting downward, crossing his wrists, he saw something zoom straight up at him.

"What...? NO!!"

"Oh, man!" Goku groaned as he soared passed Namu. "Too high!" He flipped himself around and zoomed after Namu's falling form. In seconds he closed the distance between them.

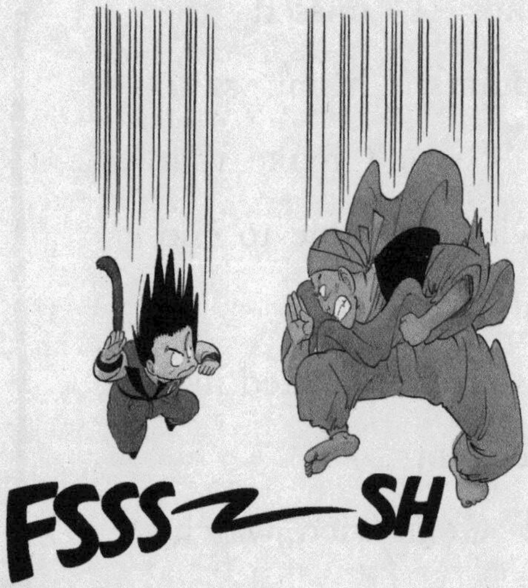
FSSS—SH

"Mind if I drop in?" he laughed.

"Ack!" Namu screamed. But he quickly recovered and their battle continued.

"A battle in the air!" the announcer shouted,

bending his neck way back to see. "This is unprecedented! Unbelievable! But most of all *uncomfortable*...for my neck!"

Namu lunged at Goku, but Goku avoided the blow by dropping lower. Namu powered after him like a rocket. Goku surged ahead, determined to land first. When Namu realized what was happening, he crossed his arms again, preparing to deliver the final blow.

"PREPARE TO BE DEFEATED!" he screamed. "THIS MATCH IS STILL *MINE*!"

But Goku had other plans. He twisted his body around so that he landed hard on his feet. He sprang back, then leapt up to meet Namu, one powerful leg extended.

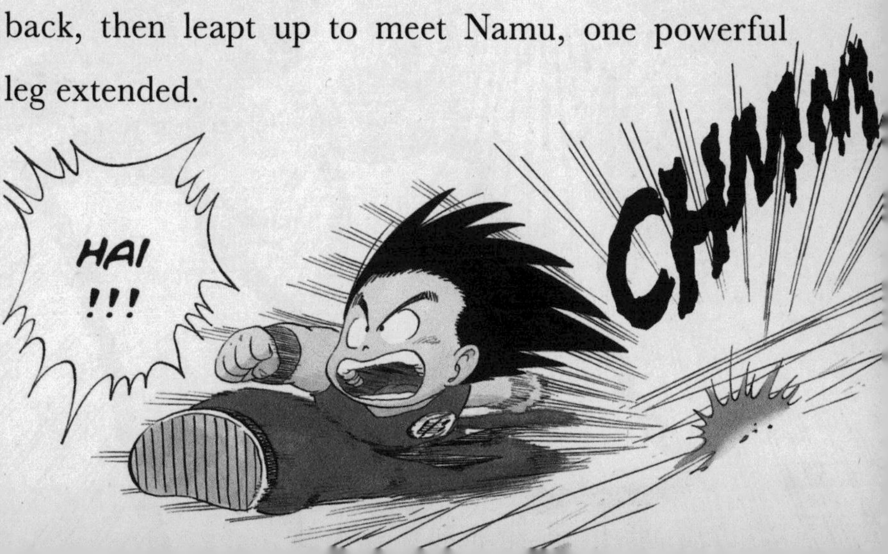
HAI !!!
CHMOM

As if in slow motion, Goku grew closer and closer until–BAM!–he slammed his foot into Namu's falling form.

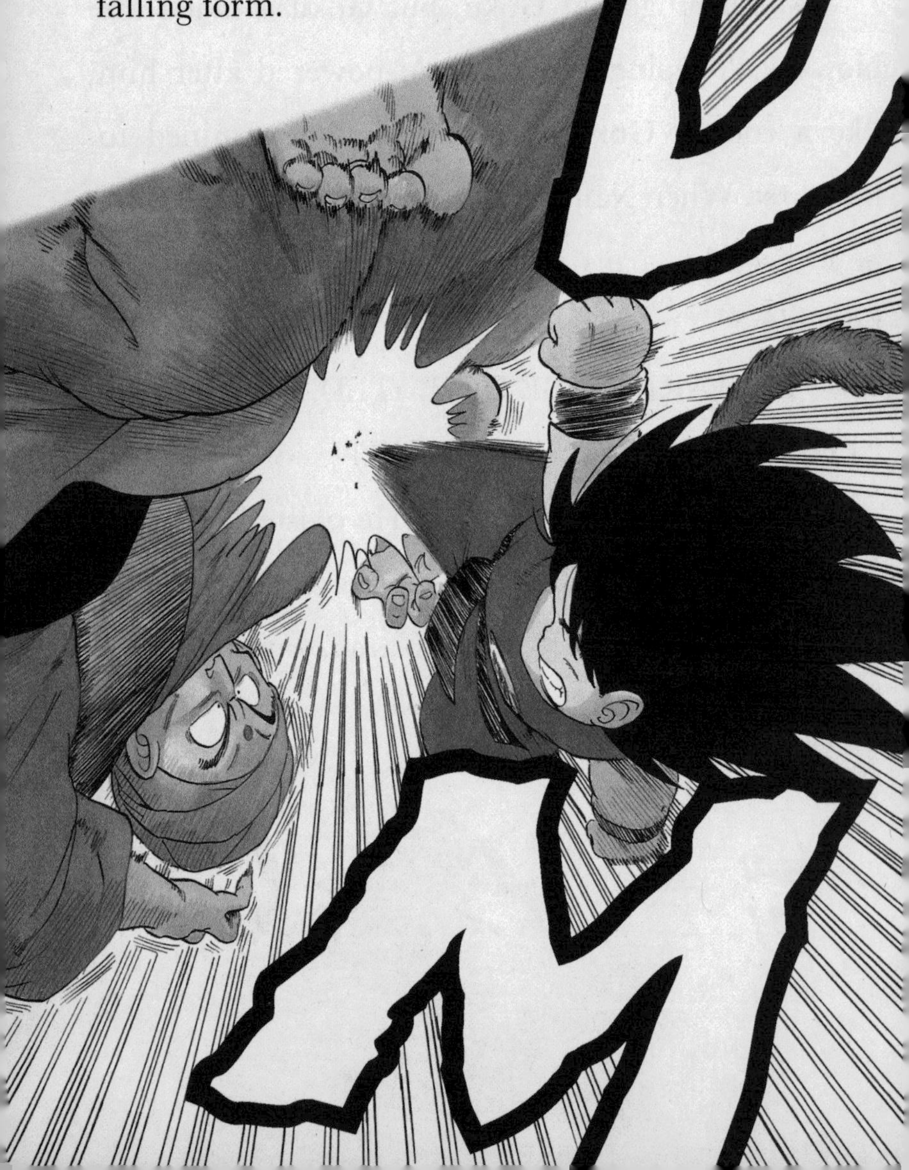

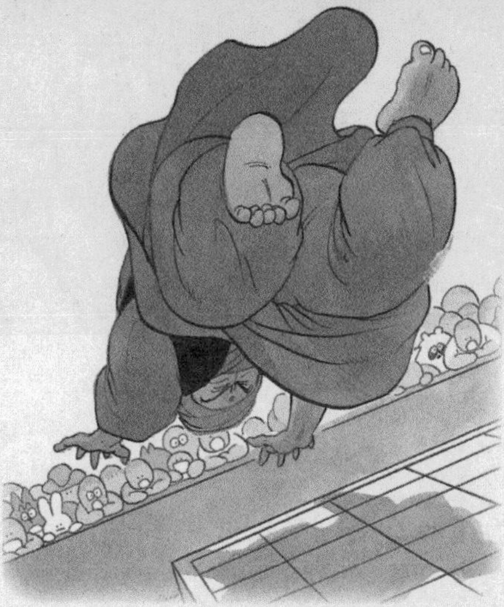

Namu

tumble

tumble

tumbled…

out of bounds.

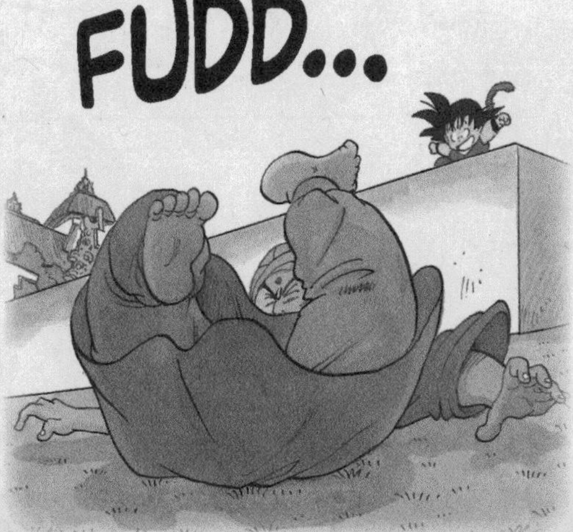
FUDD…

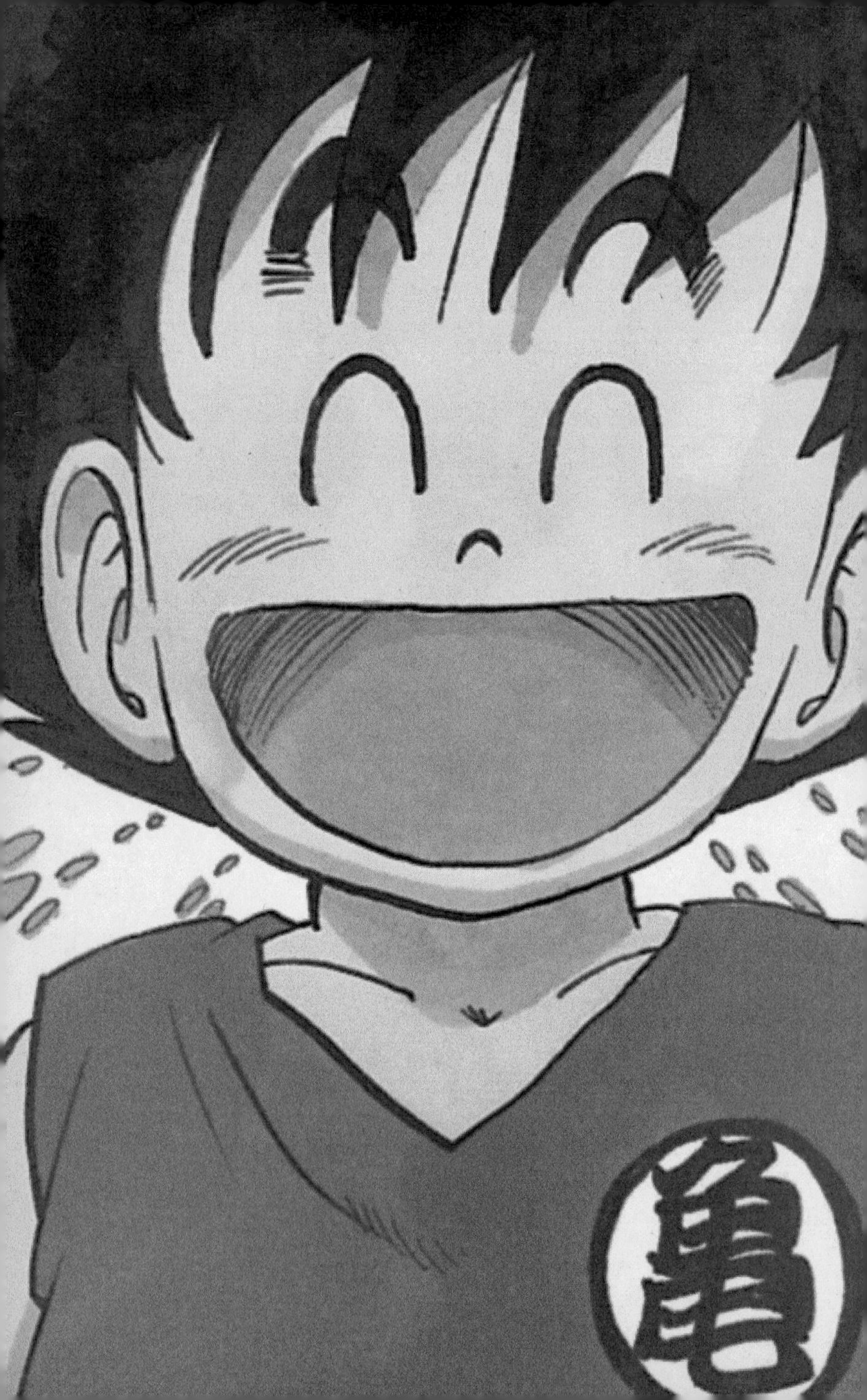
亀

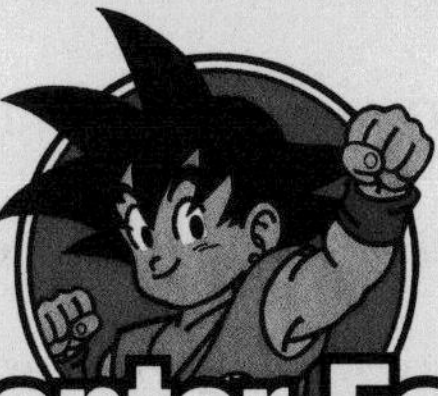

Chapter Four

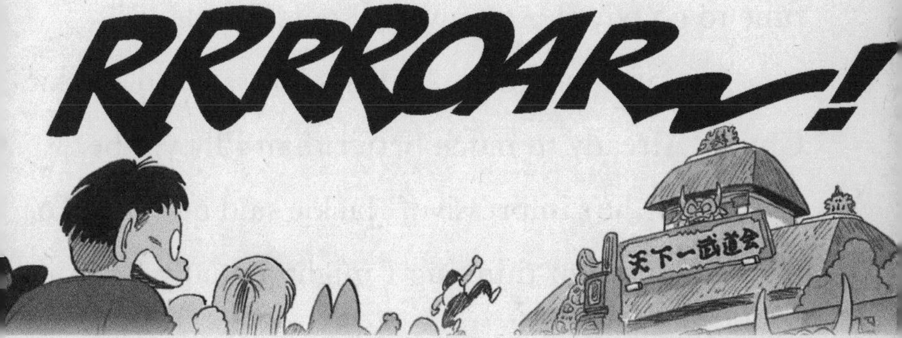
RRRROAR—!
天下一武道会

"It's *OVER*! It's *OVER*!" The announcer exclaimed over the crowd's frenzied cheers. "The most brilliant match in the history of the tournament is *OVER*! Contestant Namu has lost! And contestant Goku advances to the championship!"

Krillin slammed Goku with a huge hug. "You did it!" he cheered. "You did it!"

"You're going all the way!" Oolong yelled from the audience. "I can feel it!"

"The little lad with the big punch has done it again!" the announcer cried. "Now he will go head to head against the indescribably powerful Jackie Chun for the title of 'Strongest Under the Heavens.' But first we'll take a short intermission…the perfect time to go buy those souvenir sports bottles!"

"Goku's incredible," Yamcha said to Jackie Chun. "Already so much better than I'll ever be."

"Yes…he's impressive," Jackie said quietly. "For the first time I'm thinking I might actually lose this tournament."

As the crowd continued to cheer, Namu quietly climbed onto the fighting platform. His face was grim as ever.

"What's this?" the announcer called. "The defeated Namu is climbing back into the ring! Oooh, he looks angry! And he's heading straight for Goku!"

But when Namu came close to Goku, he smiled and extended his hand. "Congratulations, lad," he said. "I hope you win it all."

"Thanks a bunch!" Goku grinned.

Namu went to gather his few belongings and begin his long walk home. Jackie Chun watched him thoughtfully. "Not going to stay to watch the final match?" he asked.

"I wish I could, but I cannot afford to dally," Namu said. *I must hurry home,* he thought. *And tell my friends and neighbors that I failed to bring them the water they need.*

"I see," Jackie said. "Why don't you take this with you?"

Jackie tossed a tiny pellet into the air.

"A Hoi-Poi capsule," Namu said, catching it. "But why?"

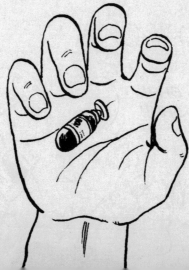

"I don't need it," Jackie shrugged. "There's nothing in it."

Namu looked confused.

"You could shrink a lot of water into it and carry it home," Jackie smiled.

"Water?" Namu asked in surprise. "Then…you know why I'm here?"

"Give me credit for a little intuition," Jackie said. "After all…I *am* the Invincible Master Roshi."

Namu gasped. "You…you really *are* the Invincib–?"

"–Shhh!" Master Roshi hissed. "I don't want anyone to know!"

"But why?"

SHH!
SHH!!

THE–THEN YOU REALLY *ARE* THE INVINCIBLE MA–

"As you know, my two students, Goku and Krillin, entered this tournament. Both of them have surpassed all my expectations; they keep getting better and better. Especially Goku with his—what should I call it?—natural instincts. Of course," he chuckled, "I don't have to tell *you* that."

Namu allowed himself a small grin.

"I wanted them to enter the contest to test their strength, but it soon became clear that they might actually have a chance of winning," Master Roshi continued. "If one of them was named Strongest Under the Heavens, he'd think he had nothing left to learn. But I want them to keep training, keep striving to become the best fighters they can be. I entered the competition to show them that there's still so *much* to learn."

"But then…why did your wig not come off when Yamcha yanked it?" Namu asked.

"It's this crazy super-strength glue," Master Roshi said. "Really itches, by the way."

“Master Roshi,” Namu said, bowing politely, “I am honored to have met you. However, I must return this Hoi-Poi capsule. You see, without the money to buy water…”

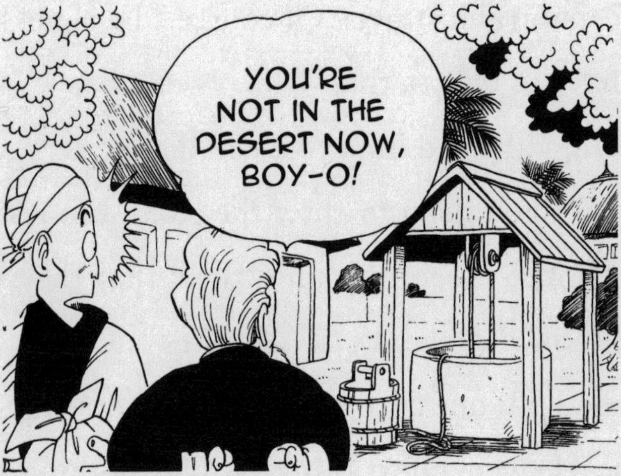
YOU'RE NOT IN THE DESERT NOW, BOY-O!

“You’re not in the desert now, boy-o! There’s so much water around here that people are eager to give it away!” He nodded toward a nearby well.

Namu couldn’t believe it. “I-it’s *free?*“ he stuttered. The announcer’s voice interrupted his shock:

“Contestants Goku and Jackie Chun, please return to the arena! The final match is about to begin!”

"Well, I'd better not miss this," the master said. "Have a good journey, Namu."

"I am so grateful to you, Master Ro—I mean, Jackie Chun!" Namu said. "If there is ever anything I can do to repay you…"

"Now that you mention it," the master said. "There *is* one little favor…"

A few minutes later, Jackie Chun strolled into the hall behind the arena, where Krillin was giving Goku a pep talk. Yamcha stepped up behind Jackie with a sly smile.

"Be careful when you fight him," he said. "It would be a shame to kill your best student!"

"How many times do I have to tell you?" Jackie snapped. "I am *not* Master Roshi!"

"Oh, give it up!" Yamcha laughed. "You can't fool me!"

"Listen," Jackie said, "if *I'm* Master Roshi… then who's *that*?"

Yamcha looked where Jackie pointed. For a minute all he could see were the faces of the countless fans filling the stadium.

Then he saw what Jackie wanted him to see. One particular fan:

A bald man with a beard wearing dark glasses and a big turtle shell.

"M-M-Master Roshi?!" Yamcha yelped. "Then…then…then you really *aren't* him?!"

"That's what I've been trying to *tell* you," Jackie said, and he sauntered toward the stage.

Yamcha immediately ran to Goku to tell him the news.

"You mean Jackie Chun's just Jackie Chun?" Goku asked.

"Well duh!" Krillin said. "Why would the legendary Master Roshi enter a tournament anyway? Everyone knows he's the greatest. What has he got to prove?"

"Then I guess there's more than *one* really tough

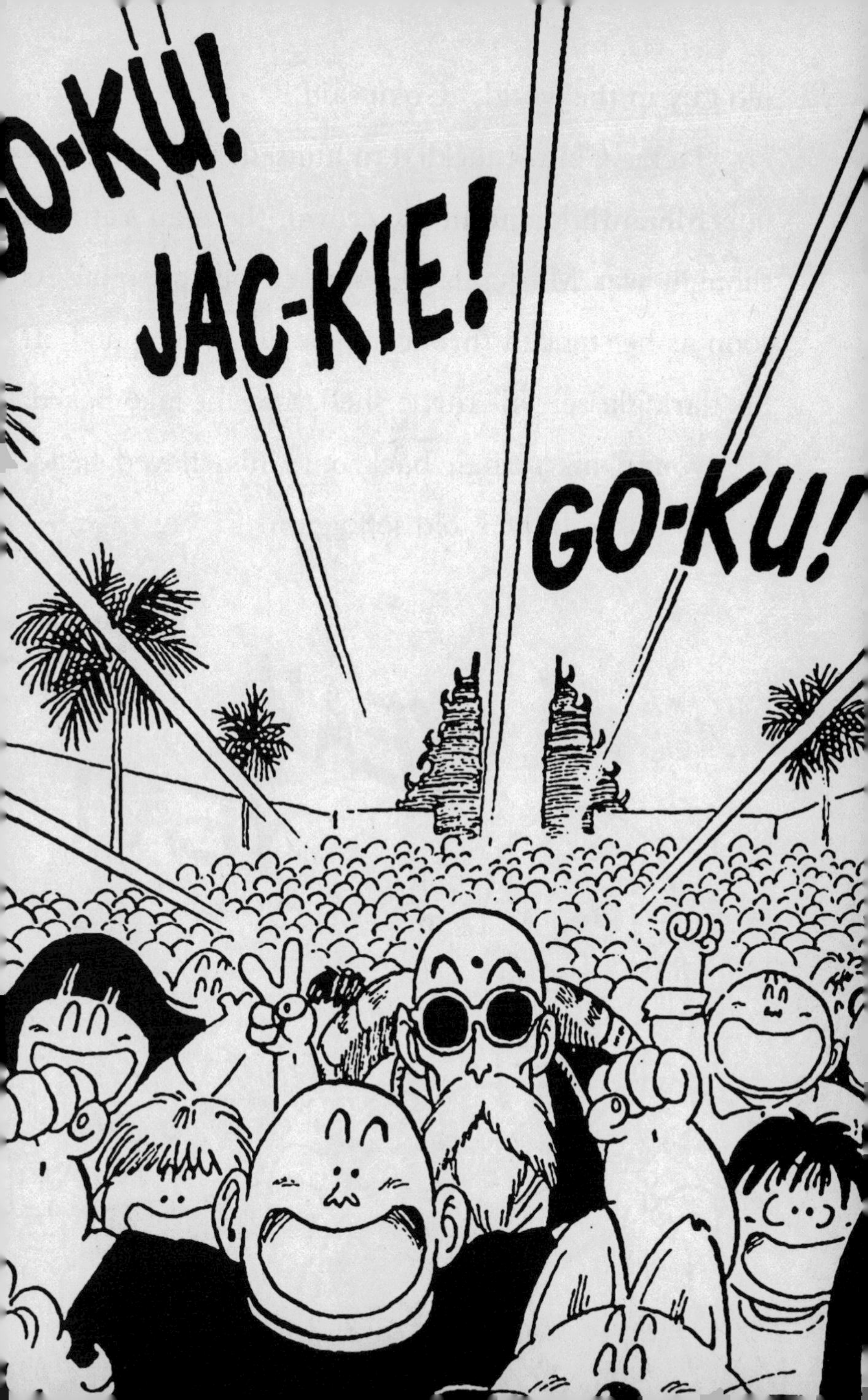
GO-KU!
JAC-KIE!
GO-KU!

old guy in the world," Goku said.

Jackie Chun chuckled to himself.

Meanwhile, out in the crowd, the man Yamcha thought was Master Roshi slipped out of sight. As soon as he stepped through the exit, he whipped off his dark glasses, his turtle shell, and his fake beard. He wound his turban back onto his shaved head. Namu looked like his old self again.

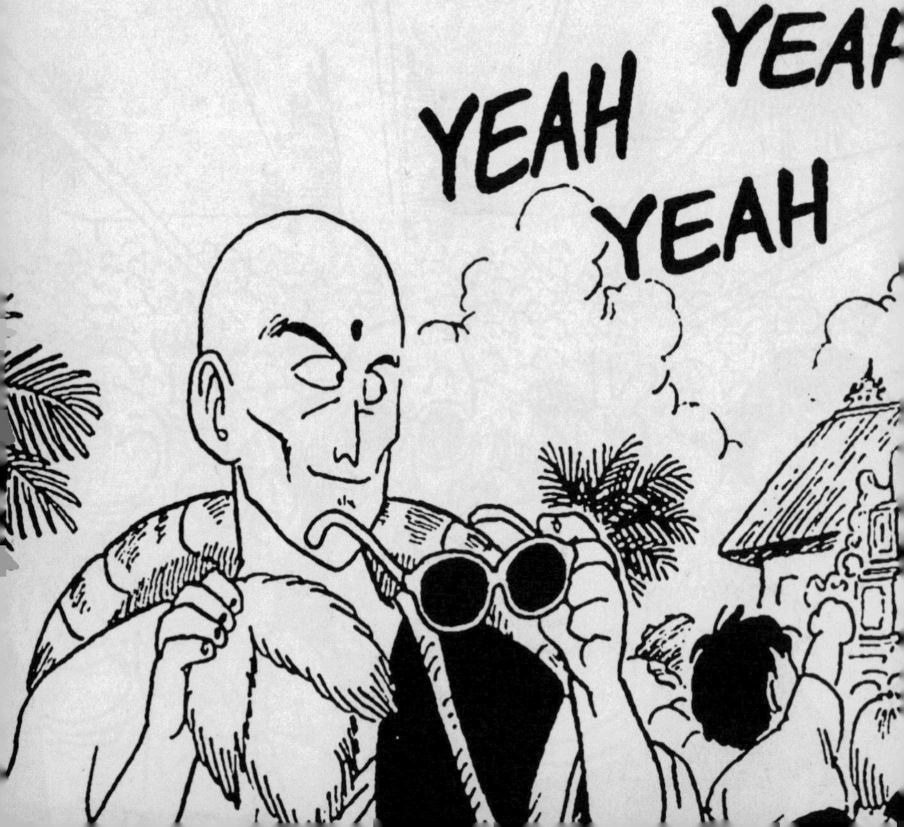
YEAH
YEAH
YEAH

I am grateful to be able to repay you, Master Roshi, he thought. *Good luck to you in your match.*

As Namu walked away from the stadium, the announcer's voice filled the air: "The final match is about to begin!"

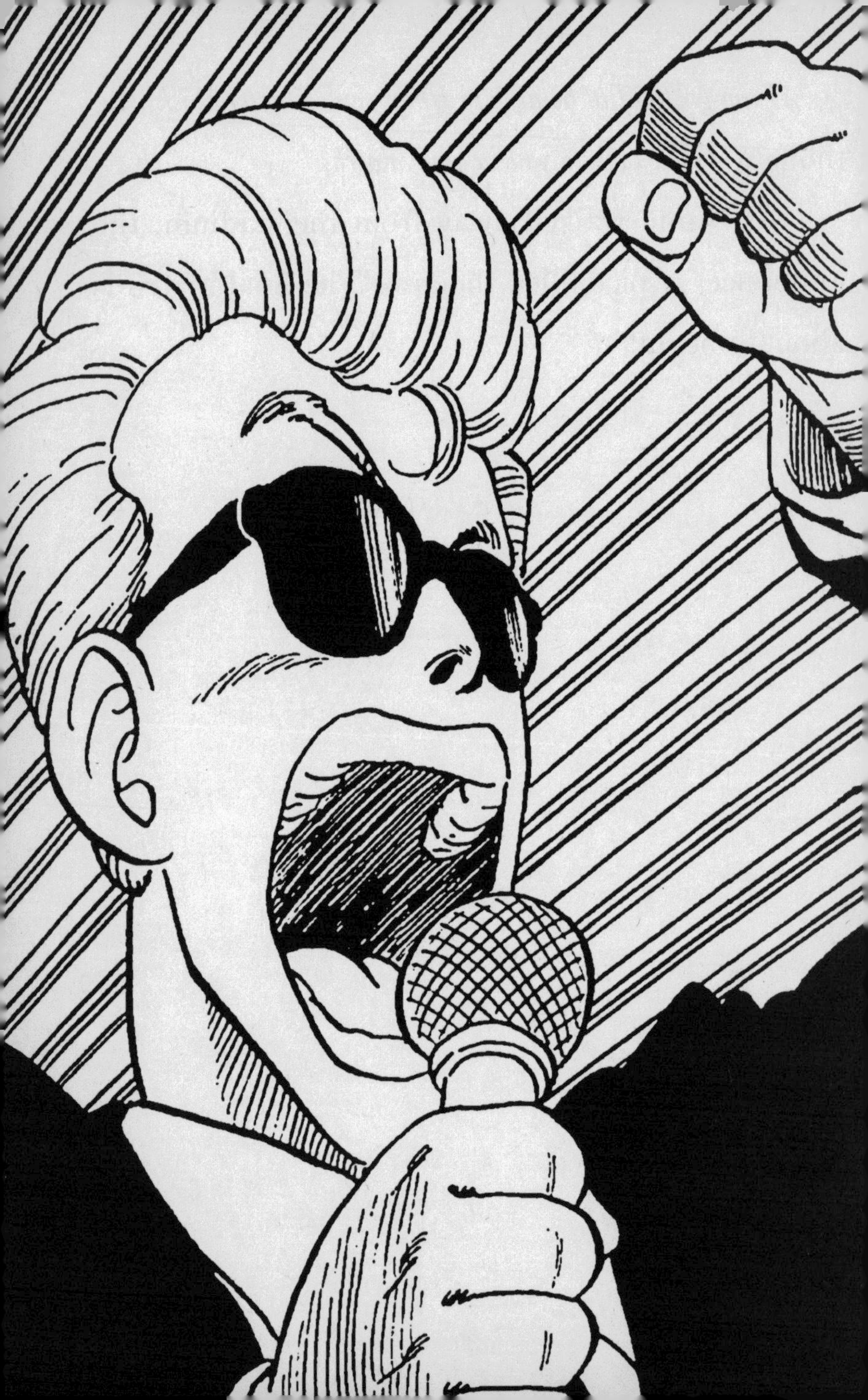

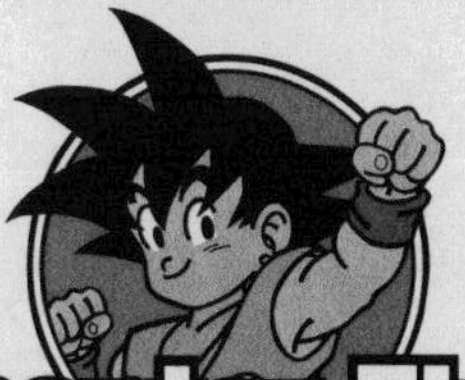

Chapter Five

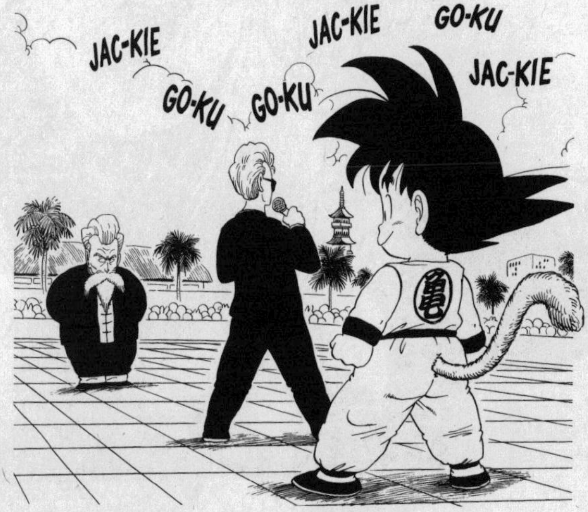
GO-KU
JAC-KIE
JAC-KIE
GO-KU
GO-KU
JAC-KIE

The crowd thundered with excitement. Goku and Jackie Chun stepped onto the stage, and the crowd roared and cheered and stomped louder than it ever had before.

"Ladies and gentlemen," the announcer said, "the moment you've been waiting for has arrived! It's a classic showdown of age vs. youth! Experience vs. strength! Average size vs. teeny-weeny-ness!

SHU...

Who will win?! Who will be named Strongest Under the Heavens?!"

He turned to Goku and announced, "In this corner...Goku!" Goku grinned broadly. "Why so smiley?" the announcer asked.

"I'm just happy to be fighting somebody so good!" Goku grinned.

SHA···

Jackie watched as the crowd cheered Goku on.

Such a wild, innocent spirit, Jackie thought. *I'll have to fight with everything I've got. For the first time in a long time.*

"The contestants will now take their combat stances!" the announcer cried.

A hush rolled over the audience.

"No holds barred, lad," Jackie said to Goku.

"You said it!" Goku answered.

"Now," the announcer roared, "let the championship BEGIN!!!"

With a mighty "HYYAAH!" Jackie lunged at Goku. Goku stood his ground until the last possible moment. Then he leapt high into the air, far out of Jackie's reach.

As Goku fell, Jackie jumped after him. In a move very like the one Goku used to defeat Namu—WHAM!—Jackie hammered Goku with a powerful kick.

Goku screamed as he soared past the arena. He flapped his arms and legs, but they were of no use. Jackie landed with a soft tap and watched as Goku sailed out of sight.

"He's going to come down out of bounds!" Yamcha wailed.

"And he's not allowed to use his flying cloud!" Krillin moaned.

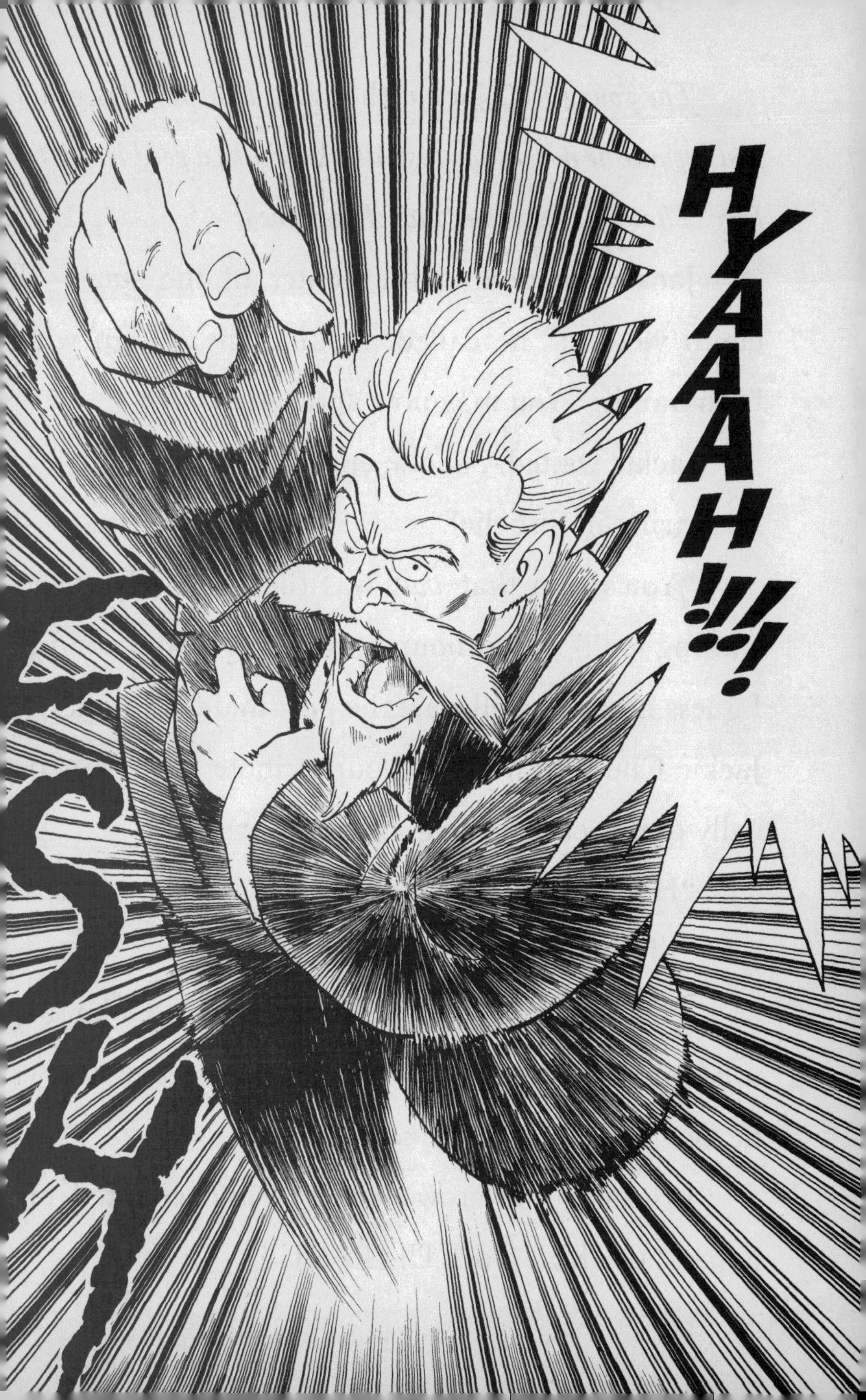
HYAAAH!!!!

The young fool, Jackie thought. *Dropping his guard just because he dodged the first attack—it'll be a good lesson for him. That was far easier than I imagined!*

Jackie stepped to the center of the stage. "I claim victory!" he called, making the V sign with both hands. "You may now applaud."

Jackie waited. No one applauded. Everyone just sat staring in disbelief.

"You mean that—*that*—was the fight we've been waiting for?!" the announcer yelled. "Two seconds?! I guess I may as well start the post-match interviews. Jackie Chun, to what do you attribute your pathetically quick, easy, boring victory over—"

"Hey!" someone called. "Look!"

"IT'S GOKU!" Oolong cried.

There in the sky above the arena was Goku, his tail spinning like a helicopter blade. He laughed as he flew back toward the stage.

Instantly, the crowd cheered and chanted his name: "Go-KU! Go-KU! Go-KU!"

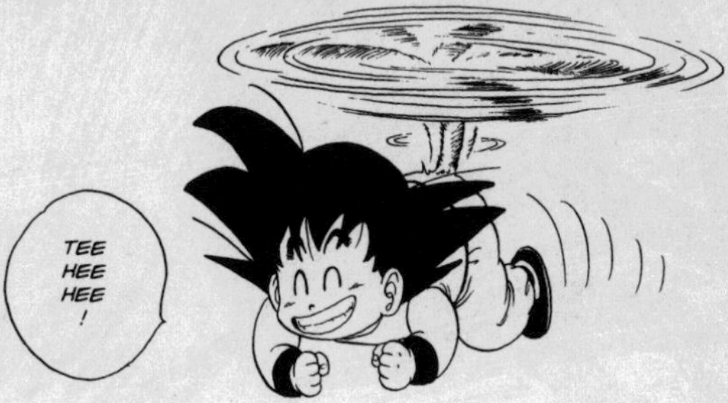
TEE
HEE
HEE
!

Jackie Chun's mouth dropped open. "I don't believe it," he breathed.

"Man, that was close, huh?" Goku grinned, dropping back to the stage. "We almost missed out on a real fight!"

"You're a lucky little monkey!" Jackie snarled. "Saved by your stupid, stupid tail!"

"I thought about using the Kamehameha to blast back, like you did, old timer," Goku said. "But I decided to save it for a special occasion."

"Insolent little brat!" Jackie snapped. "You couldn't blast a Kamehameha half as strong as mine!"

"Can too! Can too!!" Goku cried.

"Oh, you think so, do you?" Jackie said.

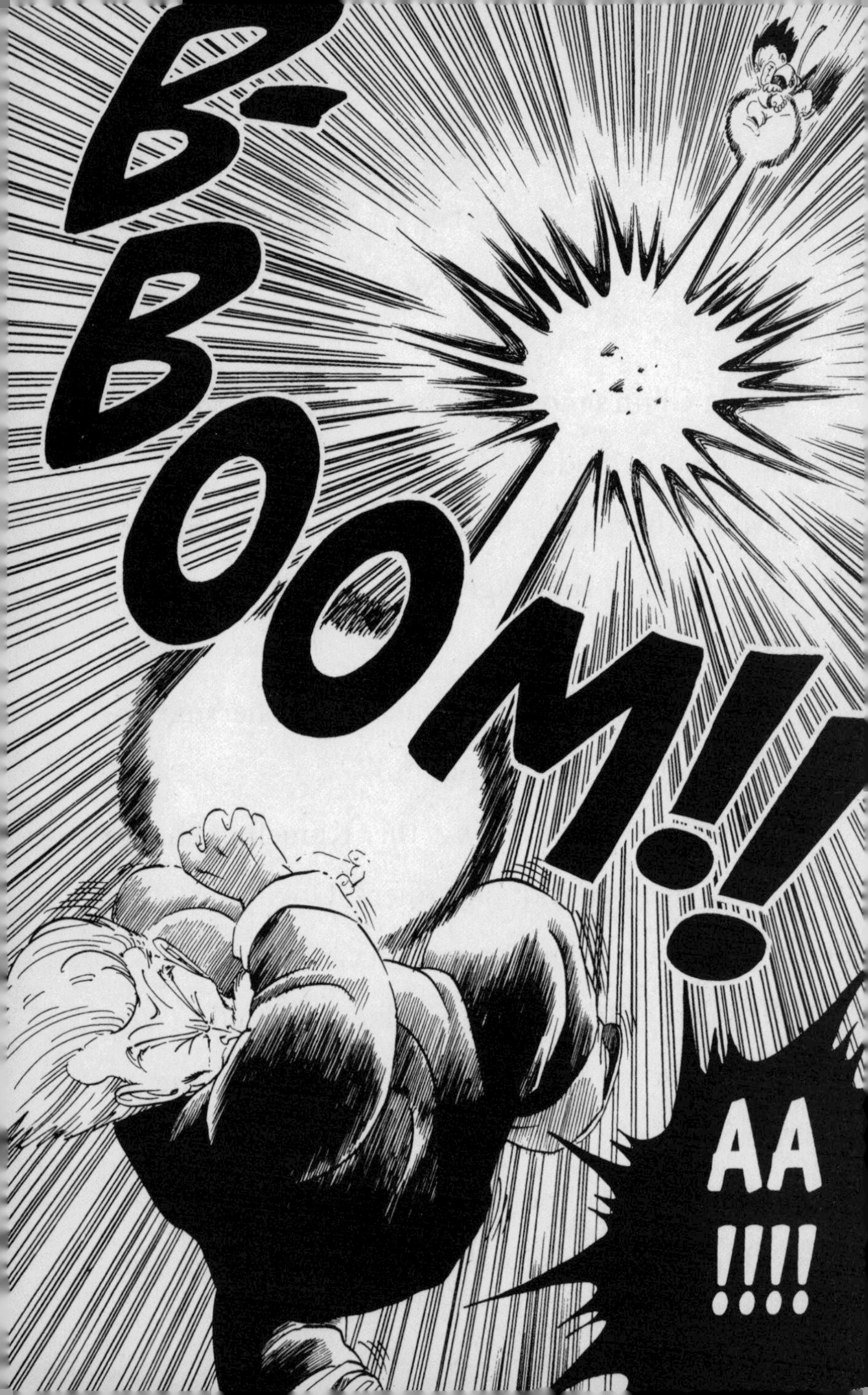
B-BOOM!!
AA !!!!

"Well, just take a look at a Kamehameha that's been decades in the making!"

Jackie linked his hands and swung them back. "Ka—" he shouted. "Me—ha—me—"

Goku linked his own hands and drew them back. He chanted a little faster to catch up with Jackie. "Ka! Me! Ha! Me!"

They whipped their hands forward, palms pointing at each other, and roared: "HAAAA!!!"

BOOM!

BOOM!

A blast of energy shot from each of them and collided midair. The stadium shook with the power. Goku was knocked to one side of the stage and Jackie to the other. Jackie looked amazed. Goku just smiled.

"We're even!" Goku said happily. "Pretty cool, huh?"

"N...no way," Jackie whispered. "No one...has ever blocked my Kamehameha..."

"Th...that was..." Yamcha said. "That was..."

"Scary," Krillin breathed.

"Another astonishing twist!" the announcer cried. "In all the world, only one person—the invincible Master Roshi—is capable of releasing the Kamehameha. Or so we thought. Today, we've seen two others unleash a Kamehameha. And one of them is a *kid*!"

Jackie Chun rose slowly to his feet. He looked more grim than ever before. *He's even better than I imagined,* he thought. *This calls for more than strength—I need a* strategy!

Chapter Six

"What a heart-stopping, breath-stealing, pulse-pounding, gut-clenching, pants-wetting thriller of a final!" the announcer yelled. "So far the fight's been even—but it looks like Goku is the one with the energy and attitude of a winner!"

"This is fun!" Goku said to Jackie with a smile. "What's your next attack?"

"Ooo, you make me mad!" Jackie said. "Just for that, monkey boy, I'm going to give you a taste of… THIS!!!"

Jackie moved so fast that he blurred, leaving an afterimage wavering in the air where he had been.

"Oh, come on, old timer!" Goku said. "I already know that trick! I used it myself, remember? If your blurry self is in front of me, then your real self must be…"

He whipped around and saw Jackie Chun standing behind him. He laughed and punched hard—but his hand went right through. It was another afterimage!

"What…?"

The real Jackie appeared behind him. "Sorry, sonny," he said. And he punted Goku across the arena.

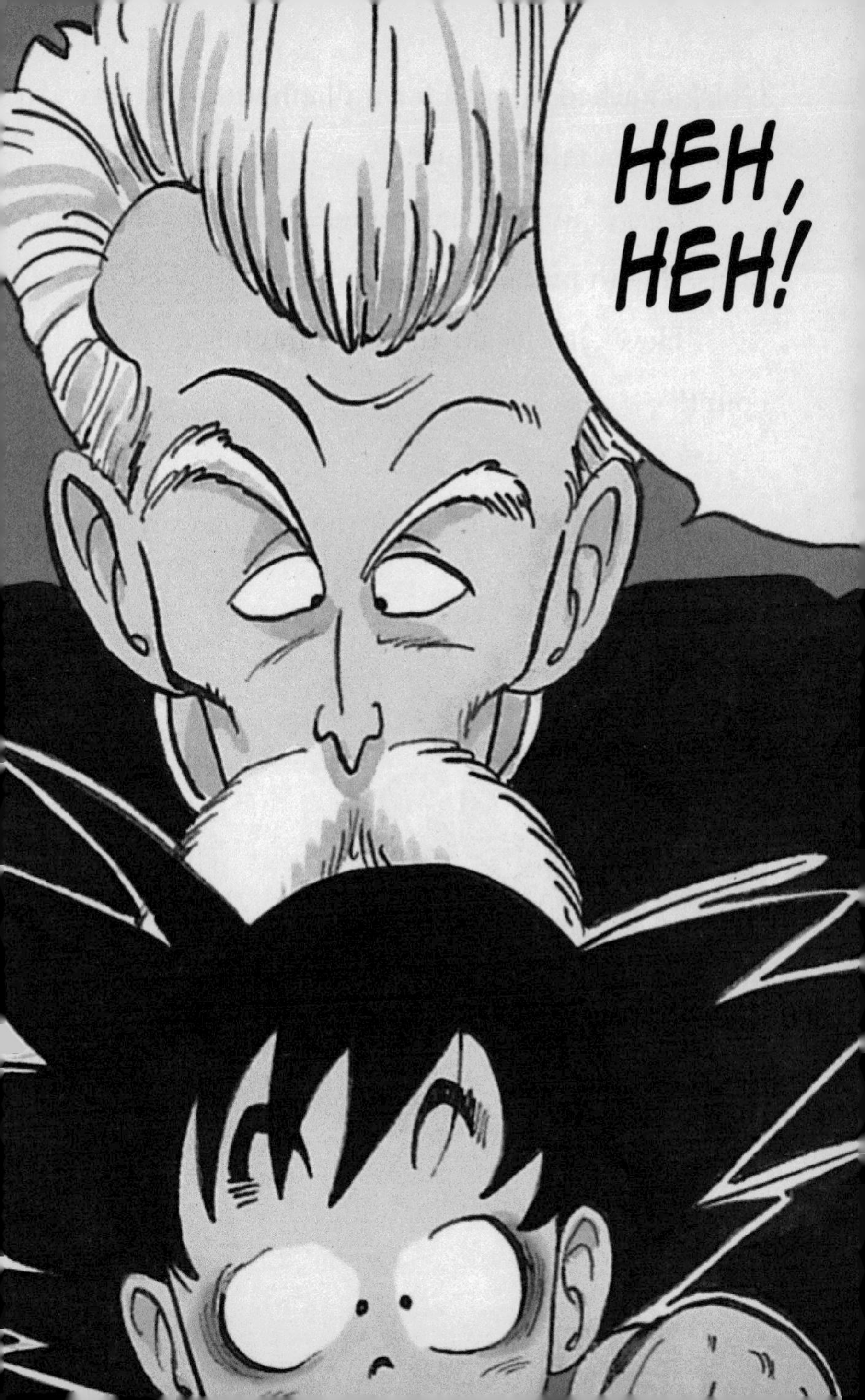
HEH, HEH!

Goku smashed into the far wall and tumbled forward in a mass of falling stone.

"*Double* afterimage attack," Jackie said, quite pleased with himself.

"Hey," he called to the announcer, "start the count!"

"One…two…thr–"

"If the kid gets up after that, I'll eat my shorts," Jackie chuckled.

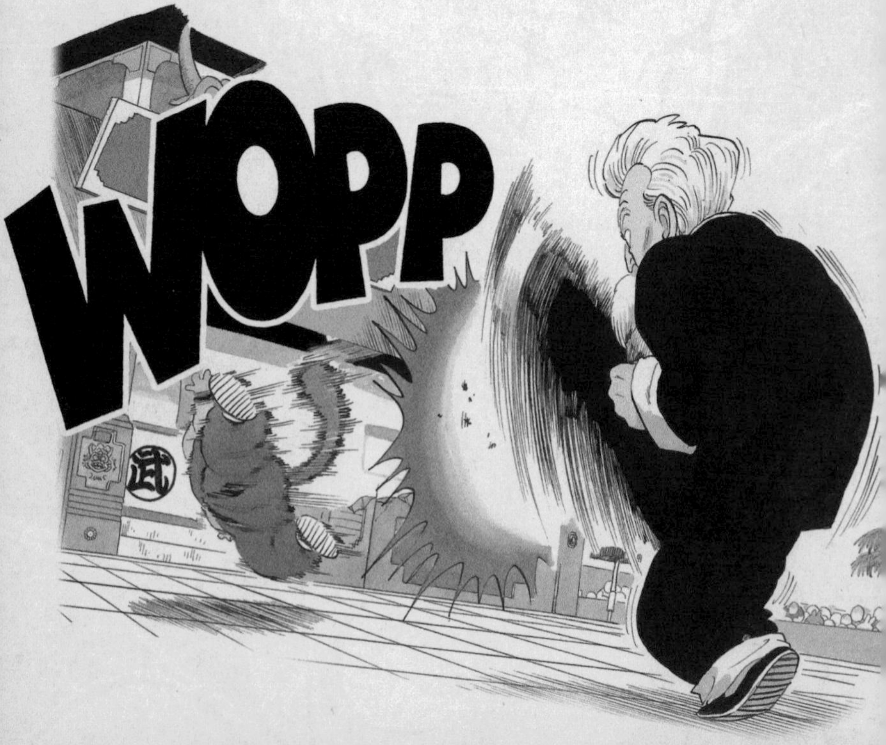
WOPP

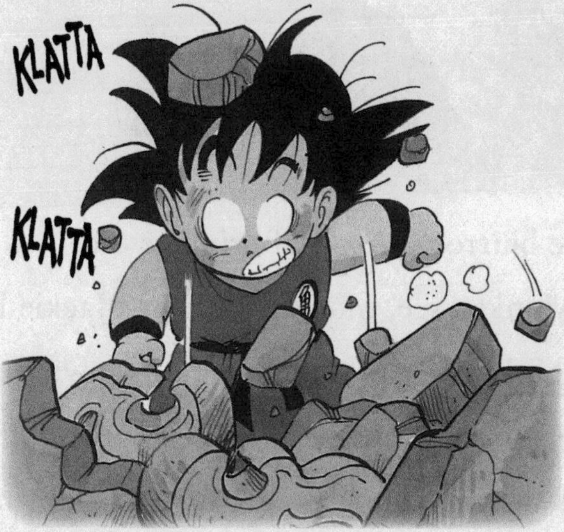
KLATTA
KLATTA

Before the announcer could finish the word "three," Goku was pushing his way out of the rubble.

"*Ptui! Peh!*" he said, spitting crumbled stone from his mouth and brushing it from his clothes. He looked up at Jackie with a smile. "You sure surprised me with that one!" he laughed.

Jackie swallowed nervously. "I hope no one heard that thing about my shorts," he mumbled.

"Now watch this!" Goku said.

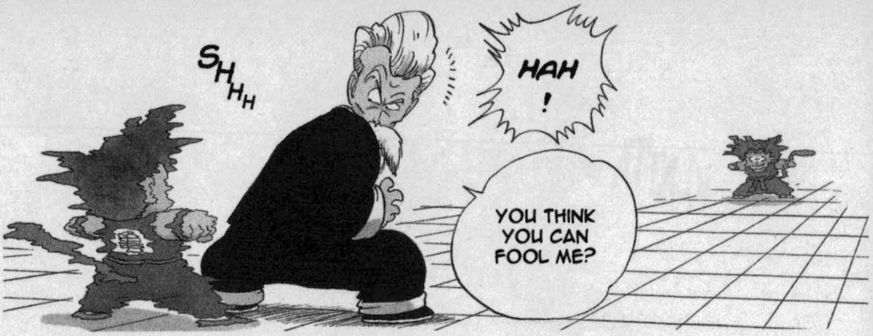
SHHH
HAH
!
YOU THINK
YOU CAN
FOOL ME?

He blurred into an afterimage too.

"Monkey see, monkey do, eh?" Jackie laughed. "You think you can fool me with my own moves?"

He looked over his shoulder where another blurry Goku image hung in the air. "An obvious double afterimage!" he said. "The real you must be..." He whipped around and saw Goku behind him. "...HERE!"

Jackie punched, but connected with nothing but air.

"No!" he gasped. In that instant, Goku dropped from above and conked the old man on the head.

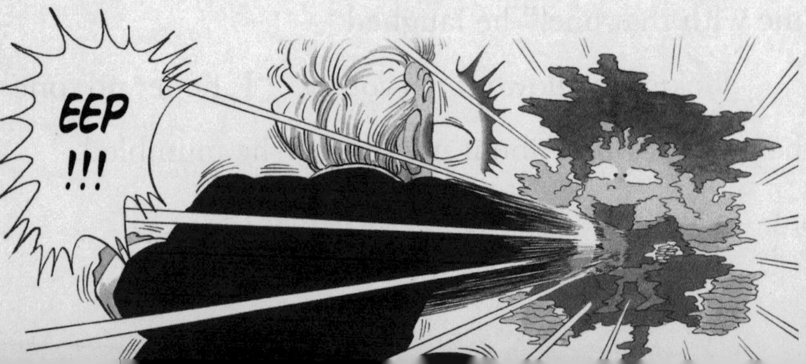
EEP
!!!

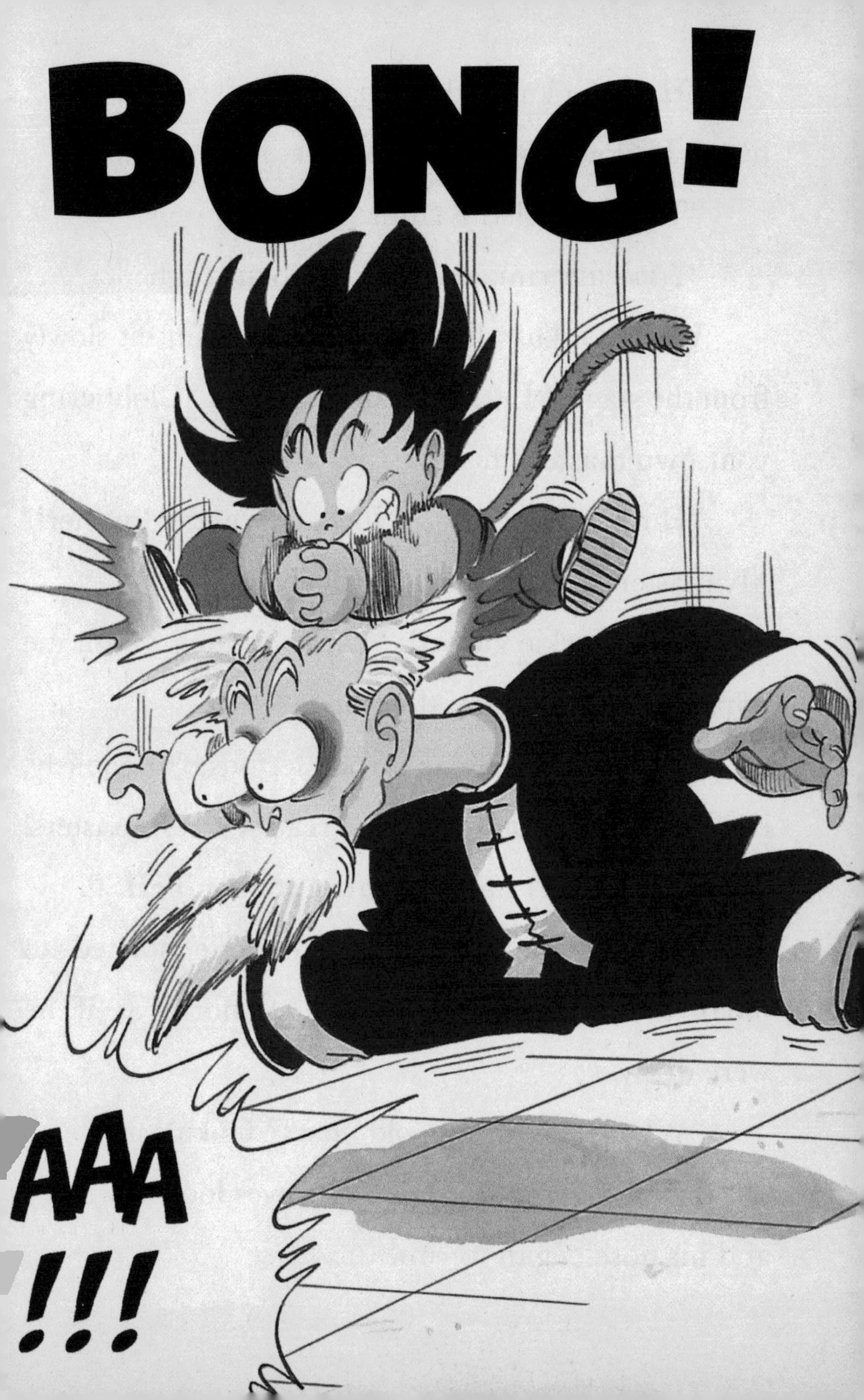
BONG!
AAA!!!

"Ha!" Goku said. "That's what you call a... hmm. If 'double' means two, what means three?"

"Triple!" yelled Krillin.

"*Triple* afterimage attack!" Goku laughed.

While Goku talked, Jackie lifted himself slowly from the stage. "Little ingrate," he said. "Clobbering your own master's head..."

"Huh?" Goku said. "How are you my 'master'? My master's the old turtle guy."

"Oh!" Jackie gasped. "Uh...you must've hit me harder than I thought! *A-ha-ha-ha!*"

In an instant, Jackie turned serious. "Obviously, boy," he said, "you have the greatest of all masters! But even he can't have prepared you for THIS!!!"

Suddenly Jackie looked pale. He started to moan and lurched around the platform as if he were dizzy.

"What's the matter, old man?" Goku asked.

Jackie started to cough. His eyes looked watery and his nose began to run.

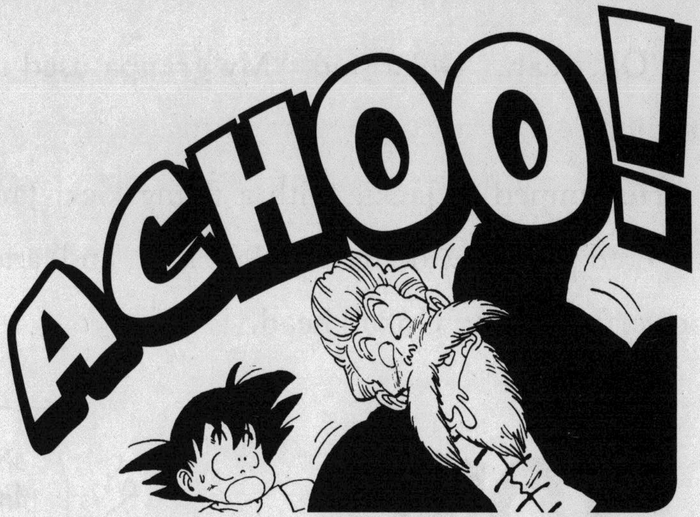
ACHOO!

"Maybe you should lie down before–" Goku started.

Jackie wiped his nose on his sleeve and conked Goku on the head.

"Hey, cut that out!" Goku said. "I can't hit a sick guy!"

"Be careful, Goku!" Yamcha yelled, trying to warn Goku "He's using–"

Jackie sneezed and kicked Goku on the chin.

Goku dropped to the mat.

"It's the Attack of the Phony Flu!" Yamcha cried.

"Oh, yeah," Goku said. "My granpa used that one a lot!"

He jumped at Jackie with a flying kick. Jackie recovered suddenly, dodged Goku's kick, and landed a powerful blow to Goku's head.

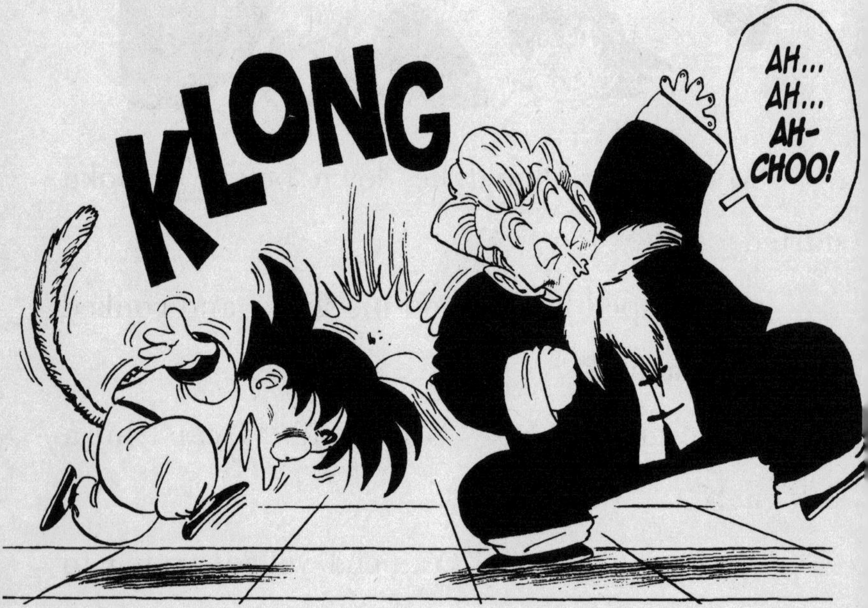
KLONG
AH... AH... AH-CHOO!

The punch shook Goku. He charged Jackie, but Jackie stepped back, and Goku missed. Jackie took the opportunity to land another kick.

Goku staggered around the arena.

"How could such a simple attack be taking such a toll on young Goku?!" the announcer yelled. "He's really feeling the blows!"

"Goku, you've got to fight!" Krillin yelled. "Don't get fancy! Just fight him like a mad dog!"

"Like a...what?" Goku asked.

Jackie charged him just then, and Goku ran to the other side of the stage.

"Ha!" Jackie barked. "You'll never beat me by running away!"

"Like a mad dog!" Krillin yelled. "You've got to be fierce!"

Goku dropped to his hands and knees. A strange sound emanated from him.

"Don't tell me I've made you *cry*," Jackie said.

Then Goku turned, still on all fours. He curled his lip, showing all his powerful teeth. He drooled and slobbered like a rabid canine. And with a mighty GGRRRRAAAWWLLL! he charged Jackie on his hands and knees.

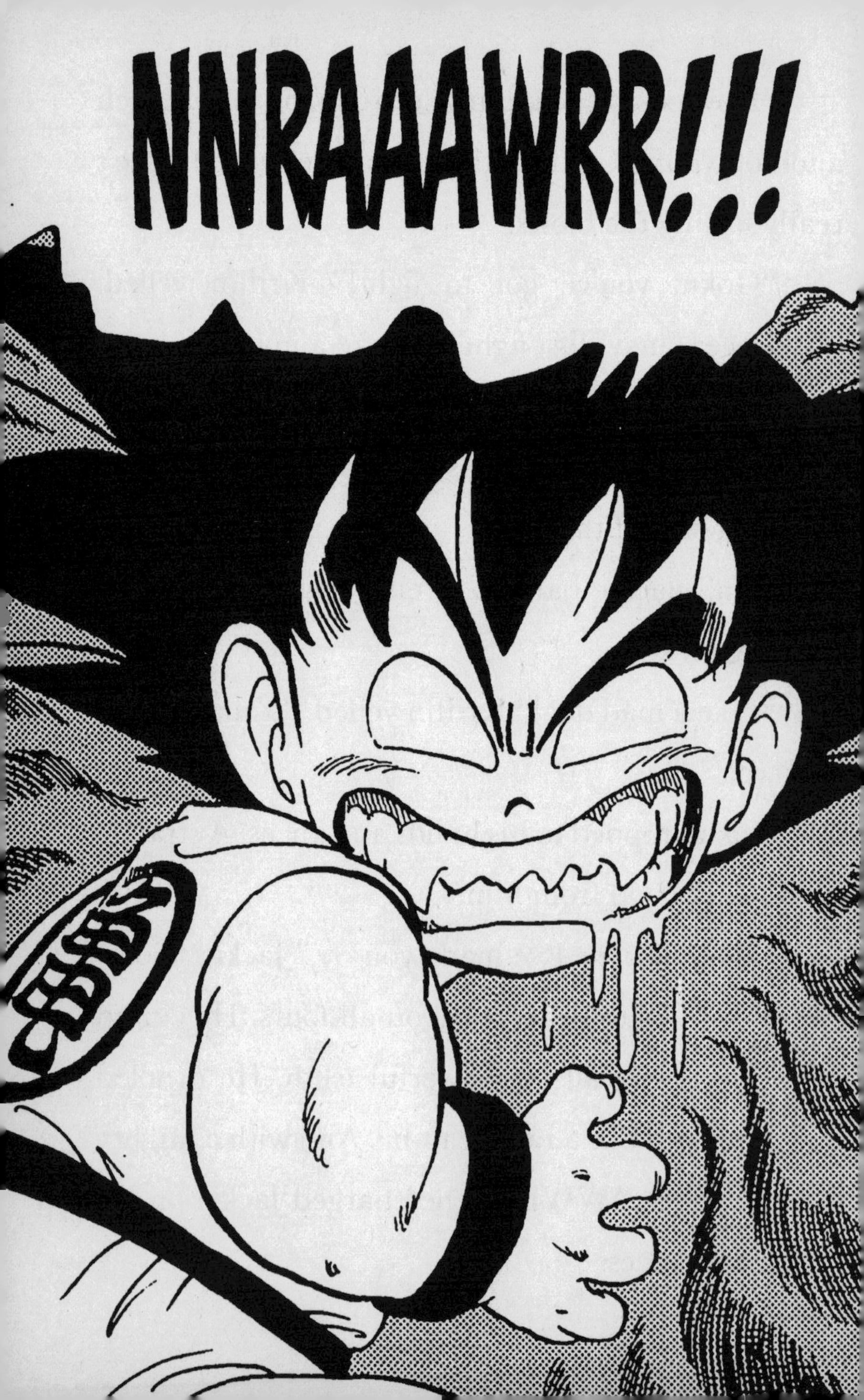
NNRAAAWRR!!!

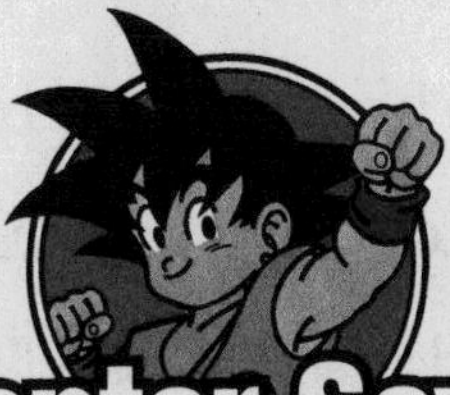

Chapter Seven

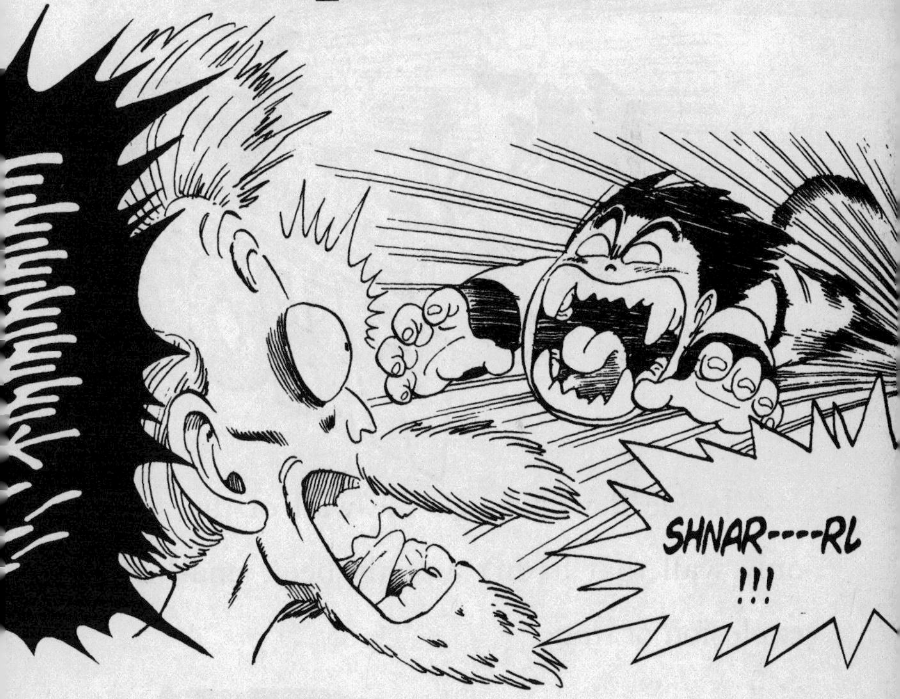
SHNAR---RL
!!!

"I didn't mean *exactly* like a mad dog," Krillin said. "I just meant–"

But before Krillin could finish his sentence, Goku jumped face-first at Jackie's throat–with his teeth bared!

Jackie braced himself for a brutal attack...but it never came. Instead, Goku somersaulted over Jackie's head and slammed his foot into Jackie's backside.

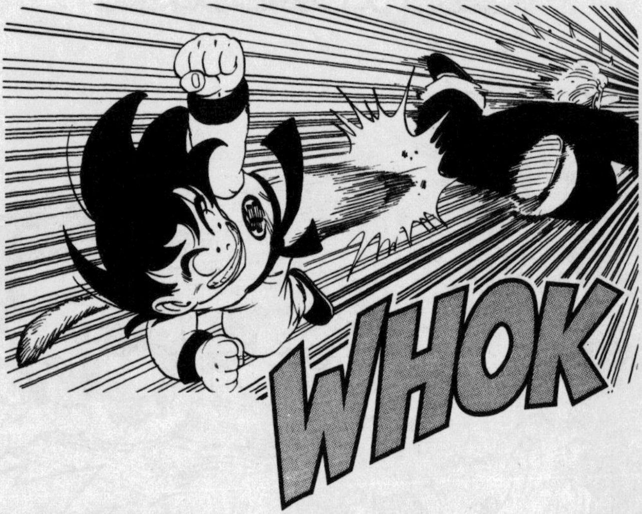
WHOK

Jackie flew through the wall of the arena–the only wall that hadn't already been smashed–in an explosion of stone.

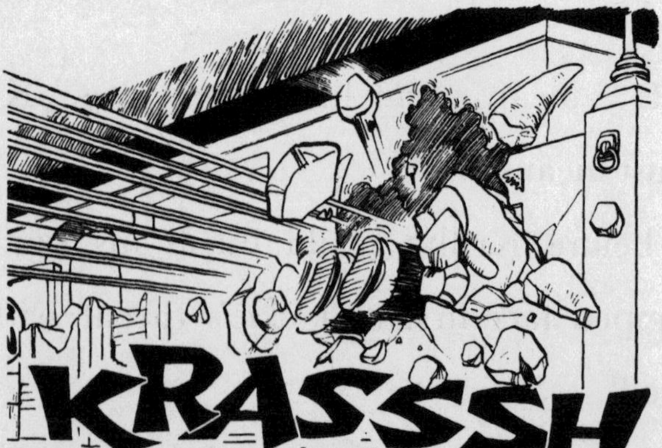
KRASSSH

Goku landed on his feet and smiled. "Hey, I just made up a new move!" he said. "What should I call it?"

"The Canine Cross-up!" Oolong called.

"The Rabid Ruse!" Bulma called.

"The Quadripedal Quick-Strike!" Pu'ar called.

"Hmmm," Goku said. "I think I'll call it… DOG FU!"

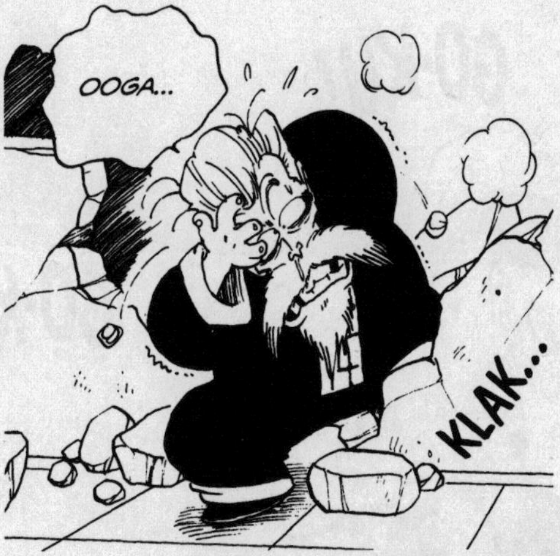
OOGA…
KLAK…

Everyone groaned. Especially Jackie, who staggered away from the wall holding his head.

"I don't like dogs," he said. "I don't like that name. And I don't like YOU!"

"What a creative fighter this young Goku is!" the announcer cried. "And what a thrilling battle he's about to win!"

"Oh, shut up," Jackie muttered. He took a step toward Goku, raising his hand to strike.

Then he stopped with his hand still raised. "You'd better not turn into a dog again," he said. "If you do, you'll *really* be sorry!"

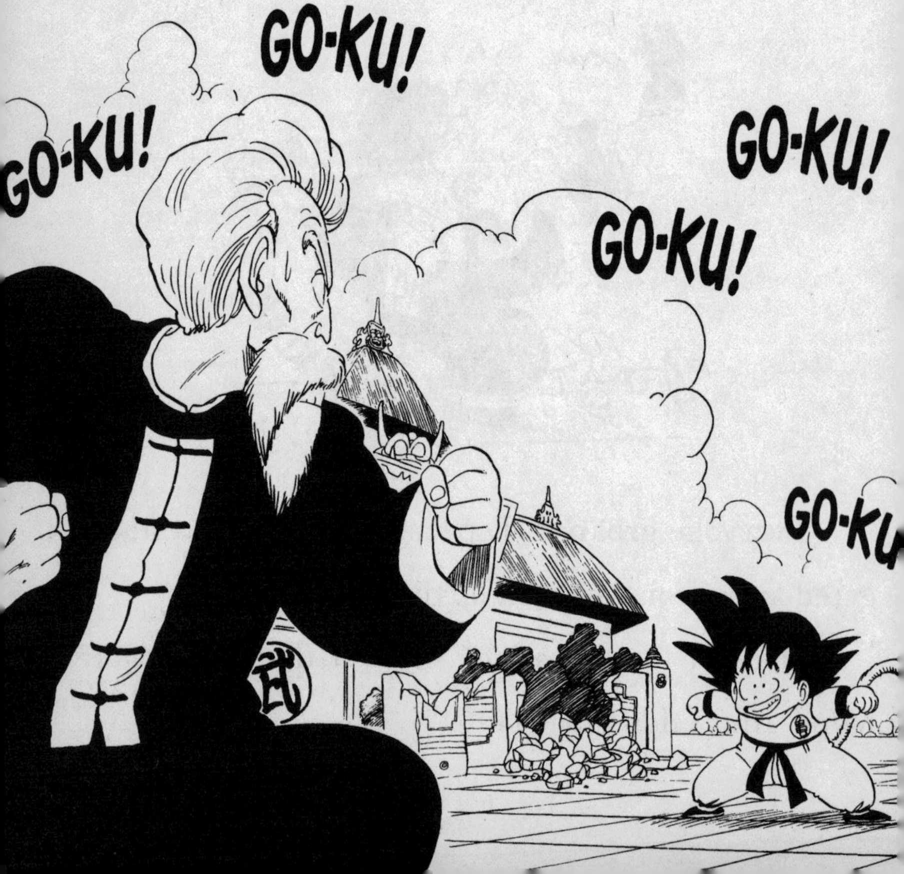
GO-KU!
GO-KU!
GO-KU!
GO-KU!
GO-KU

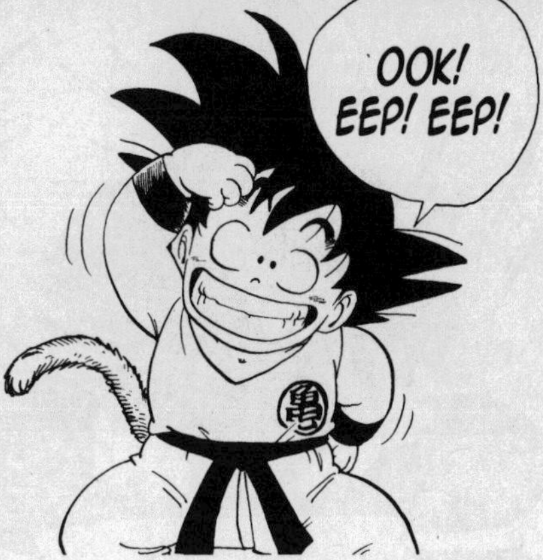
OOK!
EEP! EEP!

"Okay!" Goku said. "No more dogs!" And he immediately scratched himself like a monkey. "Ook-ook! Eep-eep!"

Infuriated, Jackie kicked wildly at Goku. Goku flipped out of the way. Jackie jabbed, Goku ducked. Then he flipped around and scratched his backside.

"Eeep!"

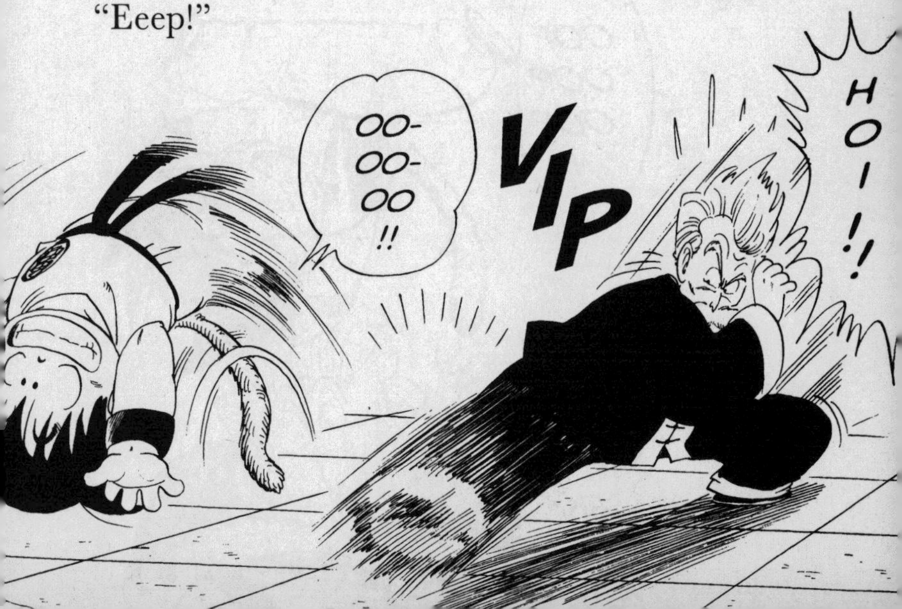
HO-!!
VIP
OO-OO-OO!!

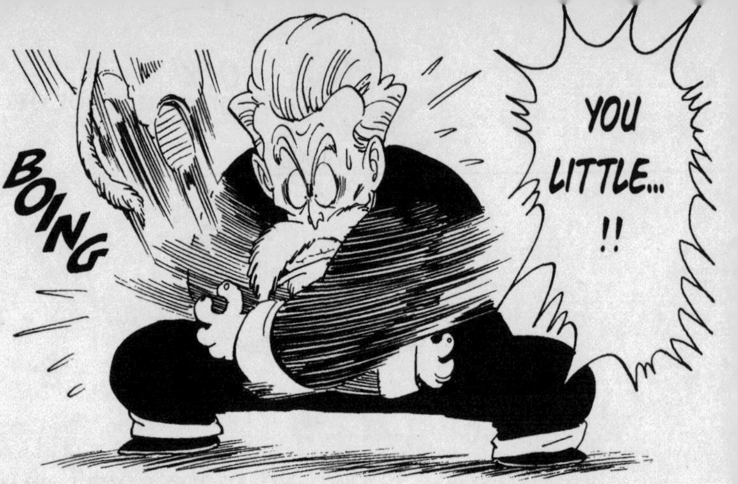
BOING
YOU LITTLE... !!

"You...you...you...you!" Jackie roared, grabbing at Goku.

Goku slipped from his grasp and landed on Jackie's head, upside down, balanced on one hand. "Ook ook!"

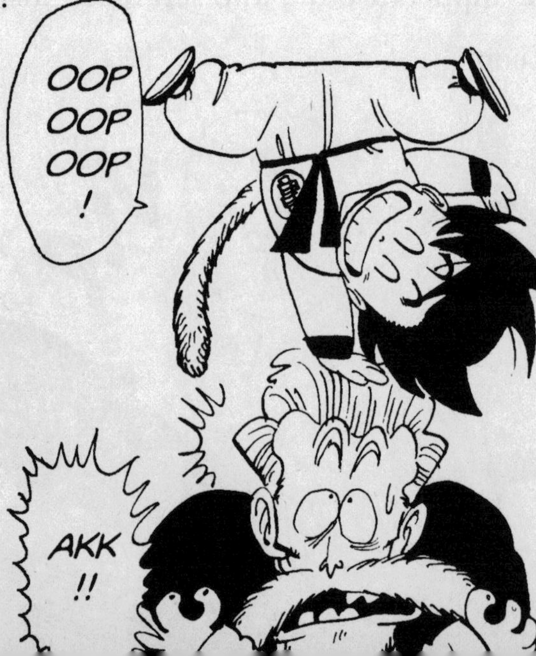
OOP OOP OOP !
AKK !!

Jackie gave a high kick, sending his foot over his head–but Goku bounded out of the way.

Then Goku made a monkey face, screeched, and jumped at Jackie's head again.

"YAAAA!" Jackie yelled.

He punched angrily at Goku. And, of course, he missed.

Goku landed at Jackie's feet and wound his tail around Jackie's ankle. "NO! NO!" Jackie yelled.

Goku jerked his tail and dumped Jackie on his back.

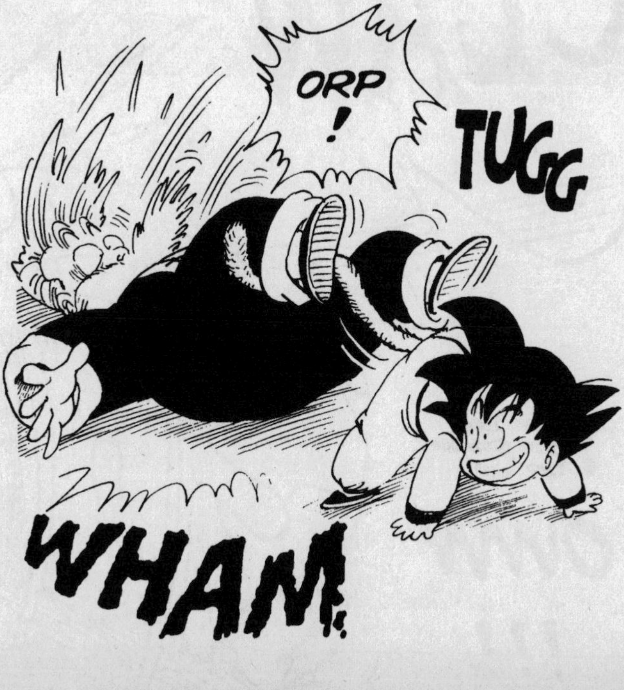
ORP!
TUGG
WHAM

Then Goku jumped onto Jackie's face and started clawing at him.

"Oop oop oop!" he screeched.

"AAARGH!" Jackie said, crawling out from under him.

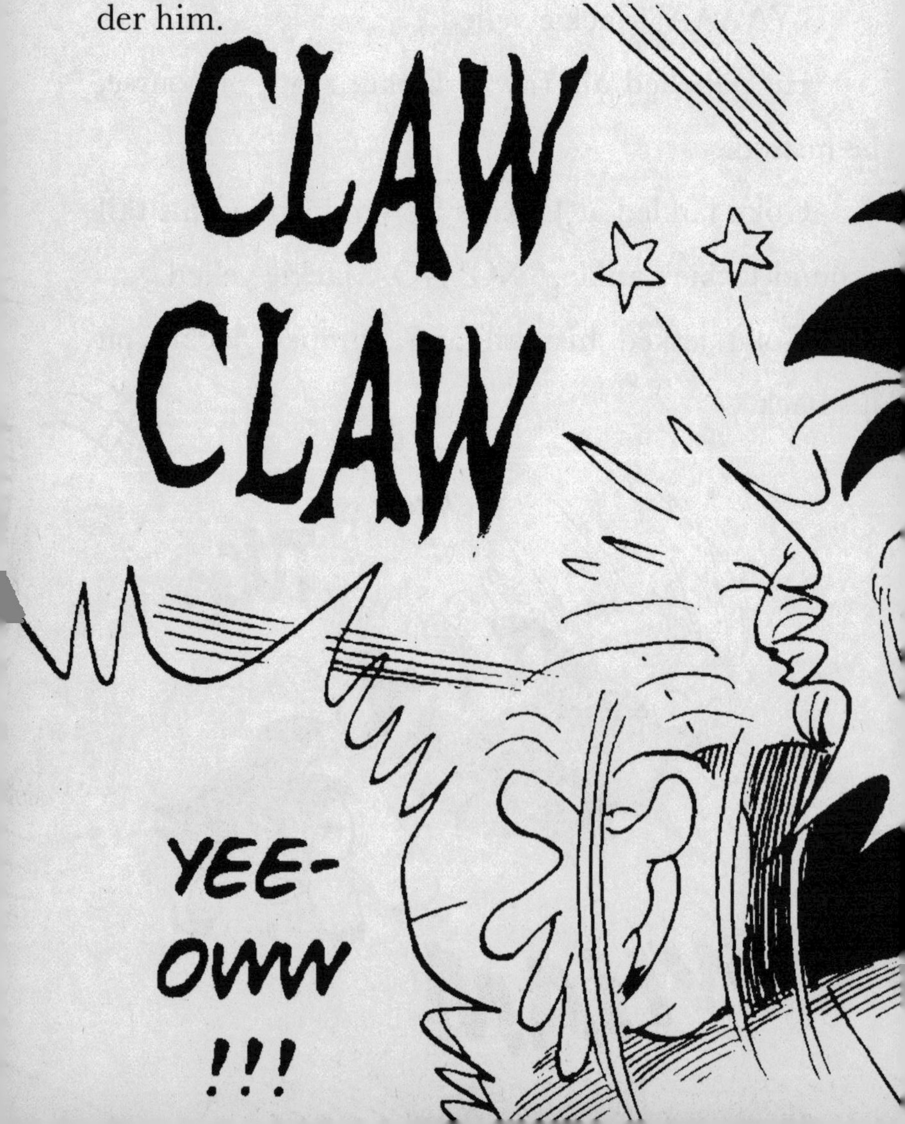
CLAW
CLAW
YEE-
OWW
!!!

"I think I'll call that one Monkey Fu!" Goku said grinning. "Eep eep!"

"Getting cocky, eh?" Jackie said. "Okay, then… you asked for it!"

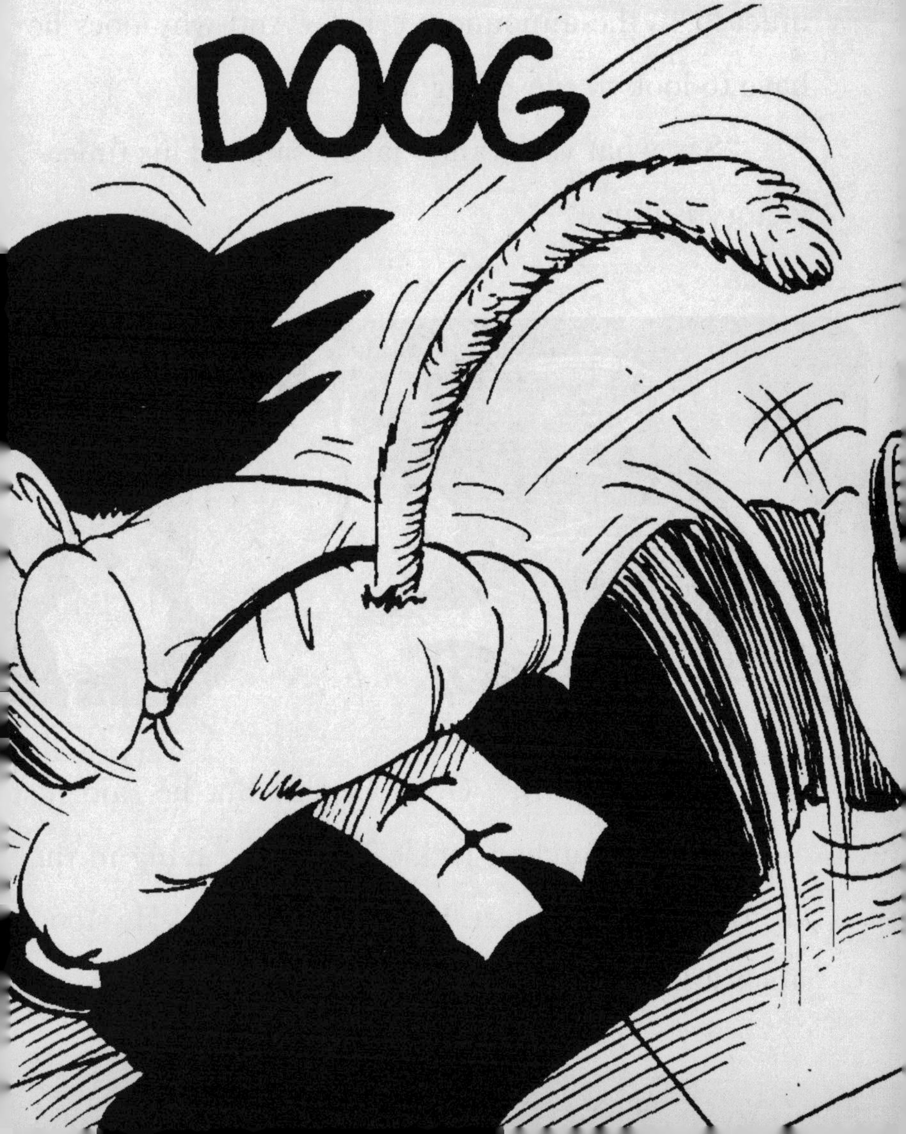
DOOG

He raised both his hands and moved them slowly through the air.

"Whazzat?" Goku asked.

"What fearsome attack is Jackie Chun about to unleash?!" the announcer cried. "And why does he have to look so *silly* doing it?!"

"Say what you want," Jackie said. "This time... victory is mine!"

"Wha...wha...?" Goku began. But he said no more. As he watched Jackie's hands weaving in the air his eyes glazed over. His jaw went slack. He stood stock-still.

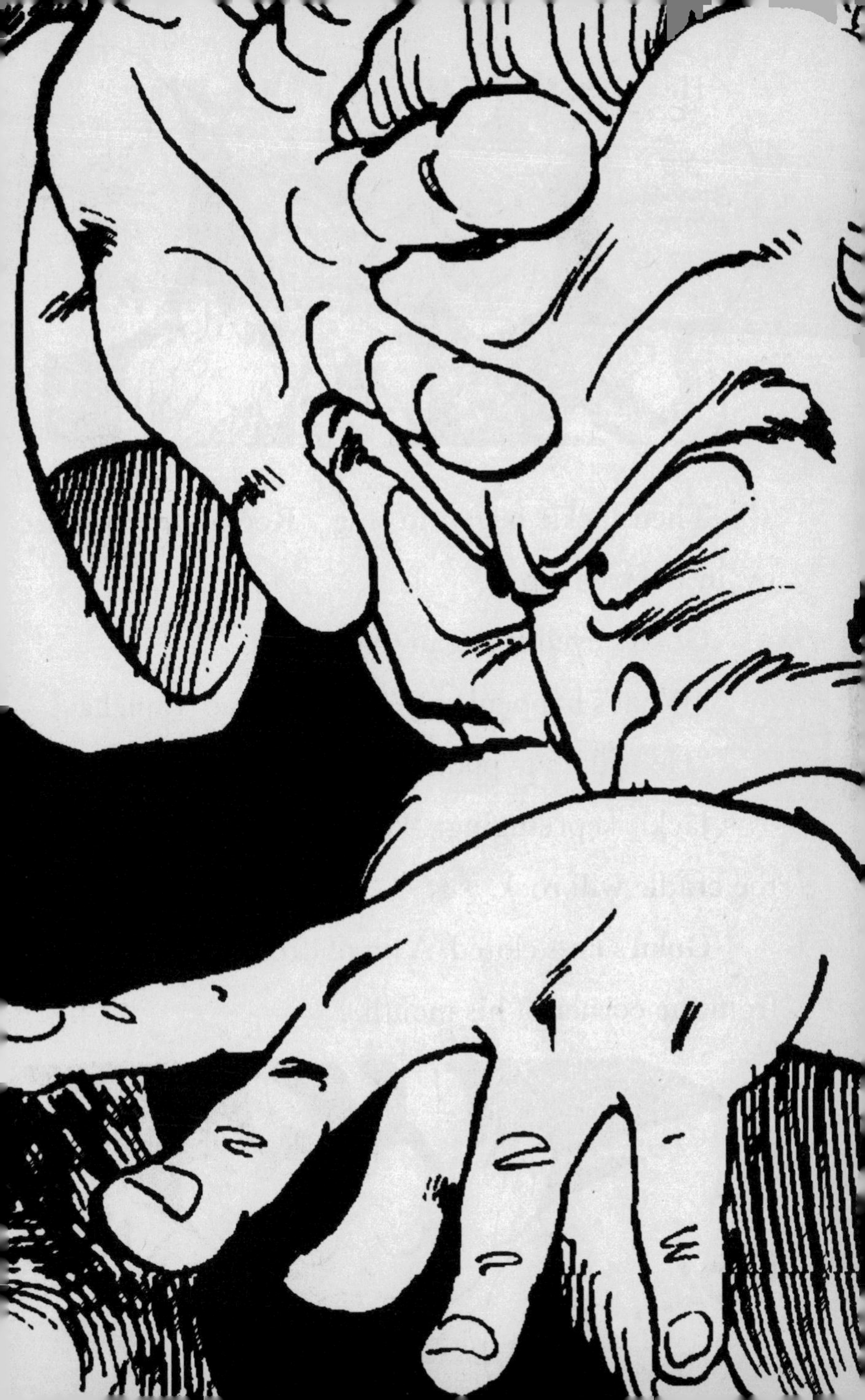

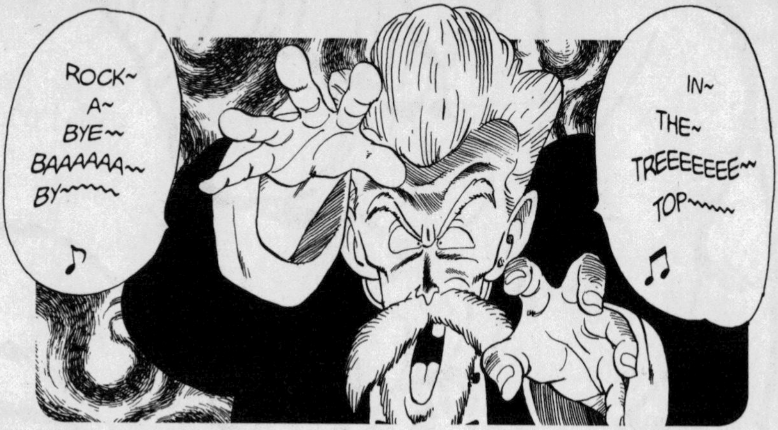
ROCK~
A~
BYE~
BAAAAAA~
BY~~~~
♪
IN~
THE~
TREEEEEEE~
TOP~~~~
♫

Then Jackie began to sing. "Rock-a-bye baaaa-by, in the tree top…"

Goku's eyelids began to droop.

"What's happening?" Krillin asked Yamcha.

"He's…he's hypnotizing him!" Yamcha said.

Jackie kept singing: "When the wind bloooooows, the cradle will rock…"

Goku's eyes closed. A bit of drool dribbled down from the corner of his mouth.

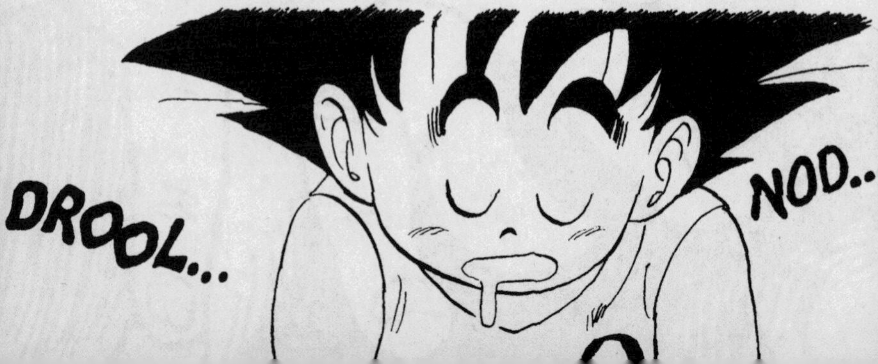
NOD..
DROOL...

And he fell forward onto the stage.

"Goku!" screamed Bulma, Oolong, and Pu'ar all together.

"Goku, what are you *doing*?!" screamed Krillin.

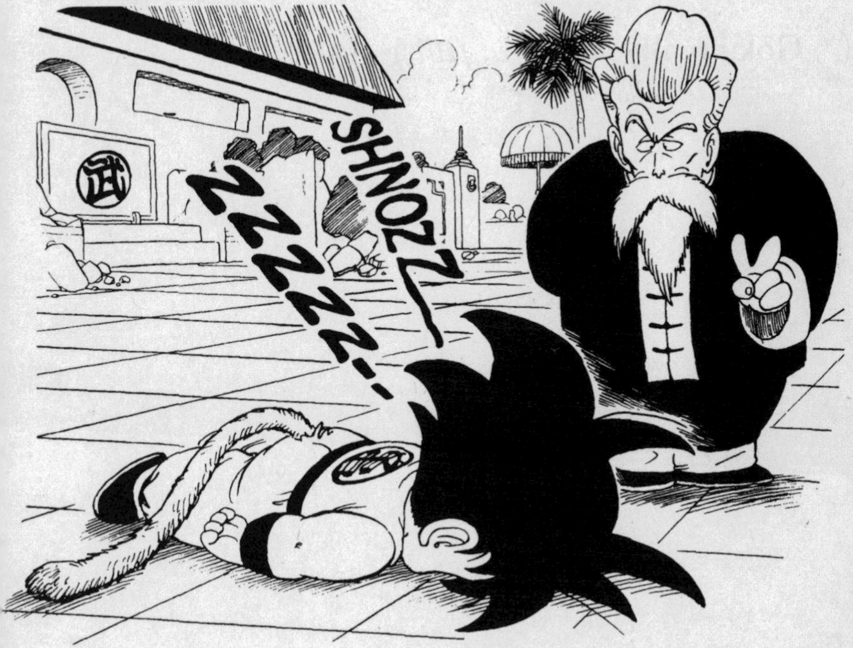
SHNOZZZZZZZ...

But Goku could only snore.

Jackie turned to the announcer with a smile. "The Nighty-Night Attack," he explained. "And with it, I've just won the championship."

The entire crowd fell absolutely silent. The announcer began to count: "One...two..."

No one could believe what they were seeing. After all that furious combat, could the tournament really end so quietly? Could the infinitely energetic Goku really lose by... *falling asleep*?

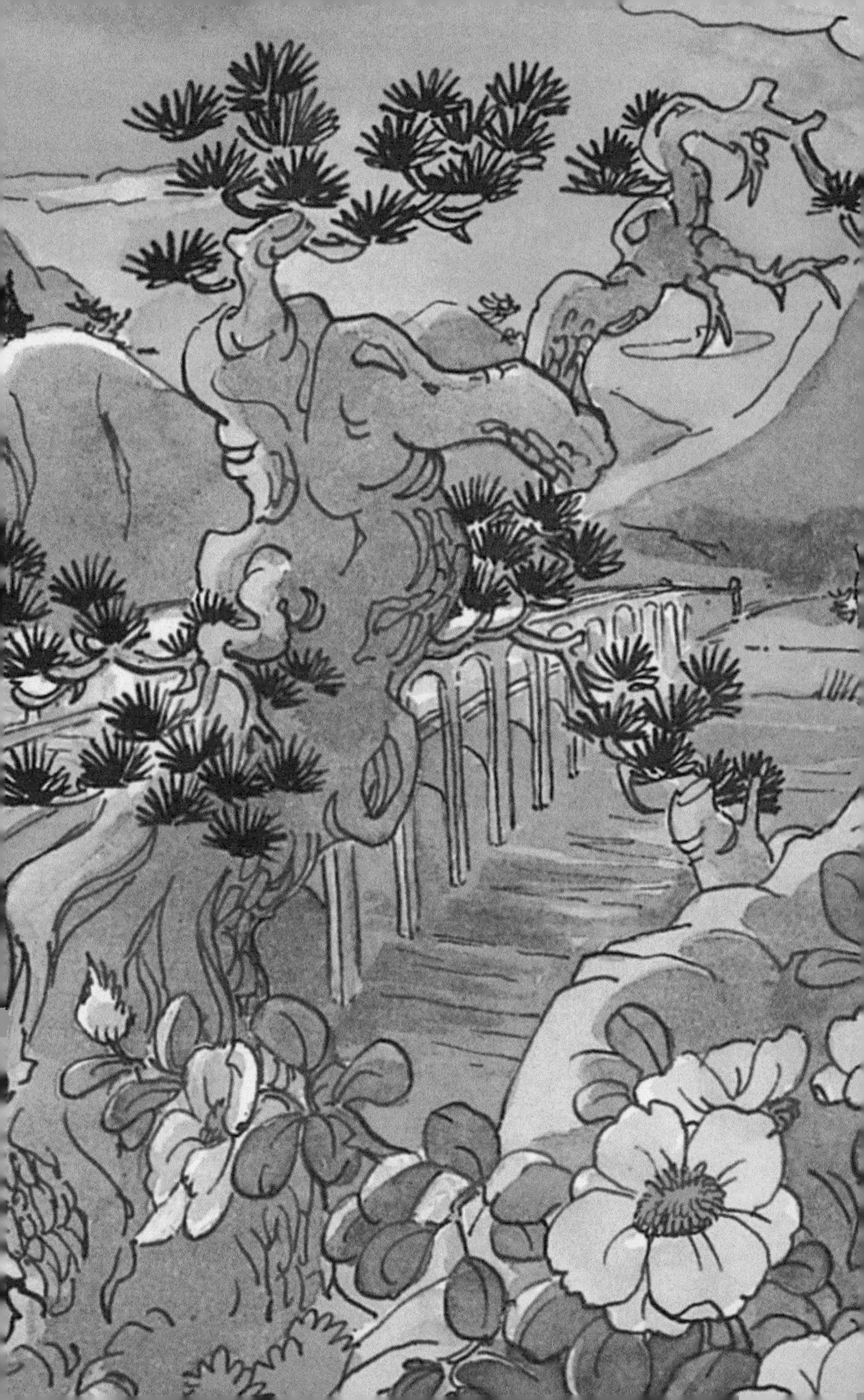

Glossary

Hoi-Poi Capsule: a tiny tube that holds any number of objects—including cars and houses—and releases these objects when thrown on the ground

Kamehameha: Master Roshi's signature move for which he summons all of his energy and focuses it into a single powerful blast

Kinto'un: a flying cloud that will carry only those who are pure of heart

A Note About Namu

You may have noticed that Namu has a dark dot on his forehead. It's likely this mark was inspired by the *tilaka*, a mark people sometimes wear to show their belief in Hinduism.

Hinduism is one of the world's oldest religions and is the third-most practiced in the world. Even people who don't believe in Hinduism are aware of its influence. For example, yoga is a Hindu practice, and karma—the idea that what goes around comes around—is a Hindu belief.

So where does the tilaka come in? Not only does the mark indicate religious devotion, but the shape, placement and color of the mark can indicate what branch of Hinduism a person belongs to. Many tilaka, like Namu's, are simple red marks on the forehead. Others are quite elaborate, include yellow, black, and white markings, and can extend the entire width of the forehead. Still others are placed on different parts of the body including the heart and stomach. Most tilaka are made from a paste mixed from sandalwood powder, clay, or ashes.

About the Authors

Akira Toriyama
Original Creator of the *Dragon Ball* Manga

Artist/writer Akira Toriyama burst onto the manga (Japanese comics) scene in 1980, with the wildly popular *Dr. Slump*, a science fiction comedy about the adventures of a mad scientist and his android daughter. In 1984 he created the beloved series *Dragon Ball,* which has been translated into many languages, and, as a series, has sold over 150 million copies in Japan. Toriyama-san lives with his family in Japan.

Gerard Jones
Dragon Ball Chapter Book Author

Gerard Jones has been adapting Japanese manga for English-speaking audiences since 1989, including the entire run of *Dragon Ball* comics for VIZ Media and the *Pokémon* comic strip for Creators Syndicate (reprinted by VIZ as *Pikachu Meets the Press*). He has also written hundreds of original comic books for Marvel, DC, and other publishers, and he is the author of several books on popular culture and children's media, including *Killing Monsters* and the Eisner Award-winning *Men of Tomorrow*. He lives in San Francisco with his wife and son, where he works and teaches at the San Francisco Writers Grotto.

Coming Soon...

Book Ten
STRONGEST UNDER THE HEAVENS

Goku and Master R–er–Jackie Chun are still at it! Seems there's nothing the old guy can dish out that Goku can't take. Well, almost nothing... But wait! What's that up in the sky? Could it be a *full moon*?

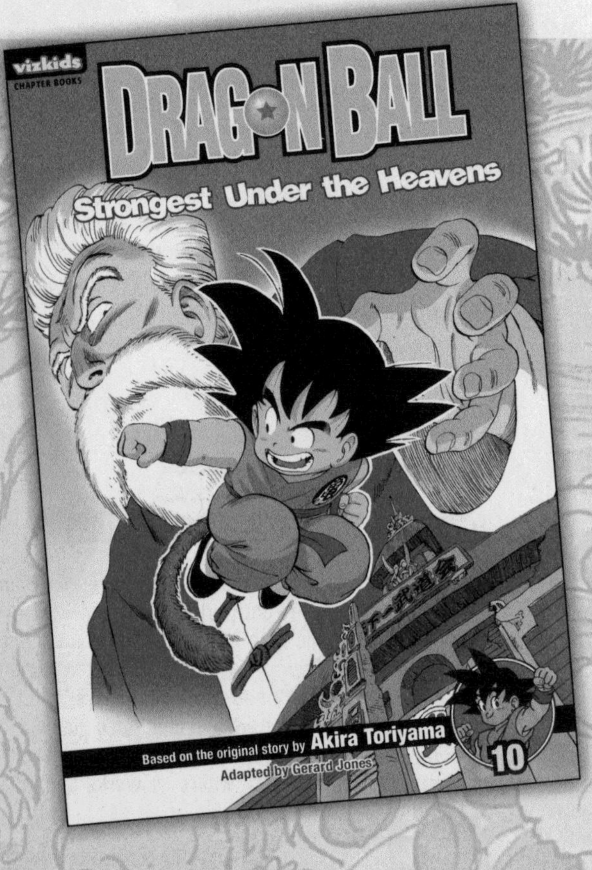
vizkids
CHAPTER BOOKS
DRAGON BALL
Strongest Under the Heavens
Based on the original story by Akira Toriyama
Adapted by Gerard Jones
10